The Hunters of Reloria trilogy series by Kasper Beaumont.

Elven Jewel

Hunters' Quest

Dragon's Revenge

Hunters' Quest

Written by Kasper Beaumont.

Cover paintings by Scott Patterson and Jaki Martinez.

This is book two in the Hunters of Reloria trilogy.

First published in 2014.

© Kasper Beaumont 2012

Edited by Bill Fox-Taylor.

Character portraits by:

Riley Malyon, John Sparks, Mae Mai Bidlake and Scott Patterson.

This book is dedicated to my clever and artistic son, Ryan.

Acknowledgements:

Thanks to Phil and Colin for believing I could do it, and to Fiona, Heav and Joanne for all your encouragement. Thank-you to Bailey for your great ideas and being my weapons' resource. My highest regards go to Scott, John, Mae Mai, Riley and Hecate for their artistry and David for the great cover layout. Bill, Sue, Joanne, Kyra and Vanessa, I'm forever in your debt for your tireless work with the editing. Thanks to year Mr Jenkinson, 7J, Heav, Wayne, Jag and Annagh for being my Beta readers.

Colin has designed a great webpage and you can go there to view some awesome artwork. There are lots more pictures and insights into the characters. Please check it out at www.huntersofreloria.weebly.com

Thank-you to Writers' Web for reviewing and publishing the first edition of this book.

Contents:

Reloria map

West Lands map

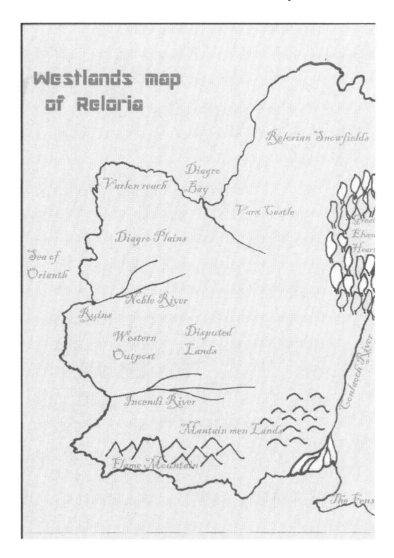

East Lands map

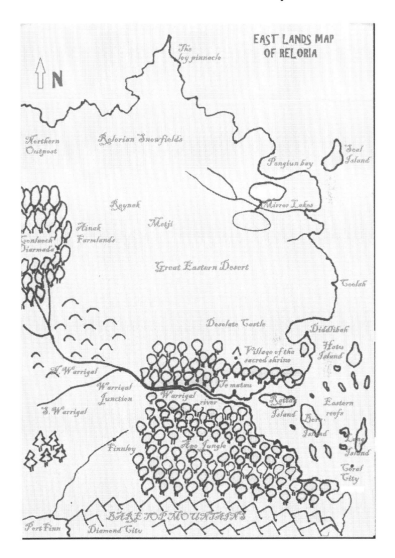

PROLOGUE

A barren moon orbits the twin worlds of Zumar and Zanarah in a figure eight pattern. As it slowly passes across the Zumaran continent of Reloria, trouble is brewing below.

Invaders from the continent of Vergash have kidnapped the Elven Princess, Shari-Rose. Her elven jewel was a key component of the Relorian shield that is the only thing preventing the Vergai hordes destroying bountiful Reloria. The force-field is now dangerously weak and the loss of one more outpost will cause it to fail.

Southern halflings Randir and Fendi witnessed the invasion by portal and together with newly-found allies, are chasing the Vergai across Reloria to find a way to the Ar'gon Tower to rescue the princess and defeat the Vergai before Reloria is overrun.

The princess was taken through the portal in the Southlands and a large battle ensued at Bamber's Brook, where the Relorians were victorious. Now the hunters travel by ship to the Eastern Outpost in the hunt for the Vergai.

This small group of allies is called the Hunters of Reloria.

THE HUNTERS OF RELORIA ARE:

Asher Grey: a rugged Mountain Man and leader of the Hunters of Reloria. His spiky hair and goatee are dark, and his eyes are a strange yellow-green. He throws knives at lightning speed and has a magical ability.

Baja Stormhammer: a happy-go-lucky dwarf who has a love for life, ale and gambling. He carries an engraved war hammer, a dragon's tooth dagger, and a small chest of coins and jewels.

Daeron: a mature guardian elf with long white hair, who carries a longsword and is the protector of the Princess.

Fendi: a cheerful halfling from Southdale and best friend to Randir. He is learning to wield his late father's sword. His bond-fairy is sweet Fendi-La.

Raja Stormhammer: a wise and thoughtful dwarf, who fights with axes and can heal with magical pan pipes.

Randir: a southern halfling who is handsome and rather clumsy. He is learning to use the longbow and has a bossy little fairy named Randir-La.

Sienna: a skilled huntress, who has tangled brown hair and wears a deep hood. Her male fairy is friendly Sienna-Li.

Sir Varnon: a knight from the Diagro Plains and leader of the knight army. He wears a tabard and steel breastplate and carries an engraved broadsword.

CHAPTER 1: SET SAIL ME HEARTIES, YO HO.

"With the sea spray in yer face

An' the glint of gold in yer ear

The mainsail's set

And it's a sure bet

We're a sight that landlubber's fear

"Through the briny blue waters we sail

With the skull and bones waving up high

From the crow's nest above

To the rat hole below

Ev'ry inch my pleasure and pride

"From the mists her barbed prow breaks

As we swoop o'er the foam

All the brigands on-board

Sing an awestricken word

For our mistress, the sea, is our home

Our mistress, the sea, is our home"

The crew of the sailing ship 'Buccaneer' finished their shanty with a loud 'Hurrah' and a jaunty solo on the fiddle as the villainous-looking seamen returned to oiling the decks and tending sails. They were a well-weathered crew, with long dread-locks covered by faded bandanas, and their salt-encrusted clothes looked to have seen better days.

The best dressed was Captain Halldor, whose dark, double-breasted jacket had gold buttons and was made of thick wool. His dark matted hair was covered by a metal helm with a line of horns protruding from the centre of his forehead to the nape of his neck. He, like his crew, carried a well-worn cutlass in a leather scabbard attached to the belt around his waist, donned shortly after leaving the quiet harbour of Port Lesslar.

Ploughing north through rough waters off the Relorian coast, the ship rose and fell through choppy waves as they navigated their way through the dangerous rocks and coral islands of the Eastern Reefs to the Warrigal River.

Huddling in the cramped space below decks, the passengers were relaxing. The dwarf Baja Stormhammer rolled his eyes at the singing, before turning back to his card game with a knight, a halfling named Randir, and two large crew members who by now were down to their last coins. The auburn-bearded dwarf was a shrewd poker player and had manipulated the game several times, allowing the unsuspecting seamen to have small wins to keep them playing. One of them smiled a black-toothed smile as he placed three queens on the table and reached across to drag the small pile of silver towards him.

Sir Varnon was a tall blond knight, whose only armour on this voyage was a steel breastplate and of course, his sword and shield, which were never far from him. Because of his years of card playing back in the Diagro Plains, he could tell that Baja was in control of almost every hand and he just played on for lack of any other distraction during the long sea voyage. In truth, the knight was missing the youthful enthusiasm of his young squire, Jacab, left behind on the Zanzi Grasslands with the rest of his army.

Only eight hunters and three fairies were on this important mission to the Eastern Outpost of Desolate Castle, where they knew invaders were coming by portal. The rest of the army was going under land through the Baretop Mountains to Conlaoch Diarmada- the great Elven City. They would warn the elves and the men of the West Lands that the Vergai warriors were coming to make war with the good people of Reloria.

As Baja shuffled the cards and the winning seaman gave a gleeful chuckle, Sir Varnon's eyes panned around the room at his companions. Their leader was Asher Grey, a secretive shape-shifter from Flame Mountain. He had led them to victory on the grassy plains of Bamber's Brook and appeared unworried by their seaward journey. As usual, his spiky black hair stuck out at all angles and he was dressed in metal-studded black leather. His yellow-green eyes glowed slightly in the dim light below the deck.

Asher stood and stretched his long arms and legs as much as he could in the cramped space. "I'll be going above deck to check on this infernal weather," he said as he followed the sailors up the companionway, a rickety ladder located between decks.

Young Randir threw in his cards, his coins all lost to more experienced players. His tiny bond-fairy had been flitting around the ship's hold and he sighed wistfully, wishing he'd seen the other players' cards through her eyes. At least then he might have a chance of winning. Randir-La smiled and flew over to share her positive energy with him.

The halfling stretched, glancing at his best friend, Fendi, who was curled up in the corner asleep, his pretty black-haired fairy in his lap.

The halfling huntress, Sienna, crouched next to him coughing gently into a large bucket. He could not see Sienna-Li, her little male fairy, but he was obviously close by, because of the halfling-fairy bond. One was never far from the other for they shared emotions and experiences. No doubt his poor stomach was heaving too.

The other two hunters were swinging in hammocks slung from wooden beams. One of them, Baja's brother Raja, was playing a low, soothing tune on his pan pipes to help ease the sea-sickness of the halflings.

Swinging next to him was a pale elf, with long white hair, who seemed unaffected by the escalating rocking of the ship, which was making the others squeamish.

Daeron was from the elven city of Conlaoch Diarmada and sometimes had visions of the elven Princess, Shari-Rose, who was imprisoned in far-off Vergash. At the moment he was fast asleep and from the smile that danced across his fine features was clearly having a pleasant dream.

Back at the poker table, the two seamen kicked their chairs backwards and left the table in a huff while Baja smiled triumphantly, raking the pile of silver coins into the engraved wooden chest that he always carried. The sailors' eyes widened at a quick glimpse of diamonds and rubies sparkling in the lamplight, before the chest was tightly latched and stowed once more under the dwarf's stocky arm. The ominous glares they cast as they climbed the rickety companionway sent a shiver down Randir's spine.

"Now will you believe me?" whispered Raja urgently into his brother's hairy ear. "If the ship's name didn't give it away, then the song most surely does. These callous fiends are undoubtedly pirates, which means we're in danger of losing the entire Princess's treasure." Raja was a well-educated dwarf from Diamond City and the thought of being aboard a pirate ship almost turned his red beard grey. Holding his head in his hands, he bemoaned the fates that had led him here.

"Raja, would you please keep your voice down," replied his brother calmly. Baja was the elder of the dwarven brothers and did not appear even slightly concerned at their predicament. "We knew the score when we came aboard. Asher bought passage for all of us hunters and surely you must have noticed Captain Halldor's gleeful look when he saw the rates being paid. He's a pirate for sure, but we are counting on his satisfaction with his exorbitant fee for our safe passage. Surely he'd be hard pressed to steal that much in a year!"

"He'll have a chance to win it back," said Baja nonchalantly. "After all, we're stuck on this ship for another week together. I'll let him win the next couple of games to appease his temper and then collect it just before we make landfall." Baja took out his treasure once more and proceeded to count the coins into piles on the table. His enjoyment was interrupted by the sound of many heavy feet coming down the companionway.

"So, what's this about you stealing coins from our shipmates?" growled Captain Halldor, a fierce pirate with a nasty scar where his nose used to be. "I think you should be handing that chest over to us for safe-keeping while aboard the Buccaneer," he added with a sneer and the hunters suddenly realised they were facing twelve pirates with cutlasses drawn.

The two seasick halflings, Fendi and Sienna quickly roused and stood as best they could on the heavily rolling deck. Their fairies surreptitiously handed them weapons behind their backs, a small broadsword and bow and arrows.

The other hunters drew their weapons and kicked the chairs aside.

 "Posts ev'ryone, a foul storm's a-brewing!" came a cry from the main deck above them as the ship shuddered violently, pummelled by increasingly heavy seas.

The pirates' paused, debating whether to heed the summons or fight their passengers for the treasure.

The hunters seized the moment to gather at the far end of the deck. Baja held a razor sharp dragon's tooth dagger, Daeron, Varnon and Fendi drew their swords, Raja an axe, and the other two halflings stood behind, clutching bows and arrows.

At a silent nod from Captain Halldor, the pirates advanced once more, yellowed teeth barred and cutlasses outstretched, and the hunters braced themselves for battle.

"You've something belonging to us," said the Captain menacingly, "hand it over and we'll let you live." He gestured with his rusty cutlass towards Baja, who was hiding behind Sir Varnon and gripping the wooden chest with one hand, his dragon tooth dagger with the other.

"Over my dead body!" shouted the dwarf while Randir and Sienna loosed their arrows into the attacking pirates. The others rushed forward, meeting amidships in a clash of metal. They were outnumbered by the pirates, but were strong fighters from their encounters with the Vergai.

Raja fought fiercely, swinging his battleaxe in a wide arc in front to prevent the pirates breaking through to the halflings behind him. Randir and Sienna managed to shoot an occasional arrow, but were hampered by the rolling motion of the storm-driven ship.

Fendi fought well against the taller pirates, ducking their unpredictable blows, while Daeron and the knight either side of him were engaging two pirates apiece.

Around the lower deck the agile fairies flitted, cutting hammocks out of the path of the hunters with tiny knives, and tangling and tripping the seasoned sailors.

Even so, the skirmish appeared to be going in the pirates' favour and the Captain called out gleefully, "I'll enjoy gutting you all like fish and taking that pretty young halfling for my prize." He gestured at the huntress busily loading an arrow in her longbow.

"Over my dead body!" yelled Fendi furiously, standing defensively in front of plucky Sienna, as she fired two arrows which narrowly missed the cocky captain.

The grizzled pirate laughed and brandished his cutlass wildly, but failed to notice Asher sneaking down the companionway behind him.

Rapidly assessing the situation, the mountain man responded by throwing three knives into Captain Halldor's back. The pirate crashed to the deck and Asher quickly leapt down, raking a knife across his throat before retrieving the other knives from Halldor's body.

Three pirates furiously charged at Asher, flattening him against the hull of the ship. He could not manoeuvre enough to throw his knives, but kicked fiercely with his steel-tipped boots.

The ship's rolling increased dangerously as the storm intensified and the fighters slid across the deck when the vessel suddenly listed to one side. The hunters grabbed for the torn hammocks to catch their balance. Voices were heard above the gale blowing above-decks:

"Shorten that sail."

"Launch the sea anchor."

"Turn her into the wind."

"Batten down the hatches."

Now the pirate crew panicked and abandoned their attack, scrambling back up the companionway to the main deck.

Randir and Daeron peered cautiously through the hatch. Sailors were rushing about trying to secure sails and rigging, but a waterspout was bearing down on the wildly rocking ship and the pirates' yelling was drowned out as a wall of water swamped the deck. Halfling and elf crashed to the floor while Asher and Sir Varnon rushed to close the hatch.

Waves crashed against the ship, rolling it flat on its starboard side for a frighteningly long time before righting itself. The wooden hull creaked and groaned with the weight of the water, and leaks appeared in the hull.

"I doubt this vessel will survive the storm," declared Sir Varnon earnestly. "We must prepare to abandon ship. We shall lash some barrels together to keep us afloat." Asher nodded and opened the hatch to the lower hold where barrels were floating in waist-deep water. Fishing several out, they tied them in pairs to form a raft.

Just as they finished, a shudder shook the stricken vessel, the main mast snapped off below decks, and a surge of water swamped the hunters, desperately trying to hang on to the barrels. Then the ship split in two with a thunderous crack and they were abruptly adrift in a wild, tumultuous sea.

"Randir, Sienna!" called Fendi in vain. White-topped waves surged at him and he was dragged under by the swirling, churning sea and unable to find his way to the surface.

The terrified halfling struggled fruitlessly in the wild sea; not knowing which way was up as he tumbled over and over. His fairy was dislodged from his pocket and swam frantically to catch up to him. Fendi tried to swim for the surface, but the dark sky made it difficult to tell up from down and he felt the air draining from his lungs. Frantically trying to find a way up through the roiling sea, he made a last desperate attempt to reach the surface, but the sky did not appear and he slowly sank into the depths of the ocean. The grey sea became white flashes of light before his eyes, then the light faded as he sank deeper in the salty water.

CHAPTER 2: SHIPWRECKED

Halfling and fairy wakened, staring up at a strange multihued ceiling. Sitting up slowly, Fendi blinked several times as he tried to recall what had happened, but his memory seemed hazy, though he had a vague recollection of swimming.

A gentle, melodic voice spoke close by. "Do not fear. You are safe here in Coral City with the mermaids."

Sitting up slowly, Fendi looked around in wonder, for he was sitting in a giant clam shell, raised on a glowing white table which seemed to float above the water, and he was surrounded by young women. He could see only their upper bodies, decorated with shells and necklaces, but they were beautiful with overly large eyes and delicately pointed features. Their long hair floating in the water was of all colours: blue, green, orange, yellow, pink and even purple.

Fendi had not heard of mermaids before and imagined it to be a term for human ladies who lived in the water.

The mermaids smiled at him and he was startled by the sight of their sharp, pointed teeth. Whatever they were, they were certainly not human and he wondered if he really was safe among them. There were gills on their necks like a fish and he surmised they probably breathed both water and air.

Glancing up again at the multihued ceiling, he wondered where this strange cave could be. The last thing he remembered was the destruction of the Buccaneer, a long way from the rocky Relorian coastline.

"Where is this place?" Fendi asked with a hint of concern in his voice, "and where are my companions?" Fendi-La fluttered beside him and small droplets of water rained down on him when the fairy shook the water from her tiny body and clothes. The little bell on the top of her pointed hat tinkled pleasantly.

"As I said, you are in the Coral City, the mermaids' home," replied a pretty mermaid with long blue hair. She carried an ornate golden sceptre with an air of authority and her voice echoed round the cavern, "We are many fathoms below the surface of the sea, in a dome made of coral."

"Coral?" asked Fendi, no wiser from the explanation. He looked at the strange knobbly patterns on the ceiling with vivid colours, as vibrant as the mermaids.

"Yes, coral. It is a bone-like plant that lives in this part of the sea. Have you never been diving around here?" Fendi shook his head, and the mermaid continued, "I am Eidothea, ruler of the mermaids and you are safe here from the storm. We will take you to land when the others waken."

Looking further around him, Fendi was relieved to discover other clam shells with his sleeping companions, but no sign of the sailors. He felt a wave of panic at the motionless form of Sienna, still wearing her hood over her brow. "Are my friends alright?"

A purple-haired mermaid gave Fendi a kiss on the cheek and giggled, "These are the ones we wanted to keep. We ate the wicked pirates for they are not good for breeding." She gave him a smile and her pointed teeth looked dangerously sharp. The mermaid put her arm around Fendi possessively as he gave an involuntary shudder. "We haven't seen a little man like you before," she said, adding, "and I like your little fairy too. When we brought you here she came along through the water as though attached to you, even in her sleep."

A golden-haired mermaid tried to wrench the halfling from purple hair's grasp and he was caught in the middle of a tug-of-war game. The little fairy flew up to the ceiling and an aqua-haired mermaid leaped into the air and tried to catch her. The mermaid's aqua tail flicked out of the water, scaly like a fish and as long as an eel with two barbed forked ends. The giggling mermaid hit the water with a splash, showering Fendi, but the blue-haired mermaid leader pointed her sceptre at the aqua mermaid and a jet of water sent her sprawling across the cavern. "Be still!" commanded Eidothea.

Fendi was frightened by these strange and aggressive creatures and called out to the sleeping elf who was the closest to him, "Daeron, please wake up. We've been kidnapped!"

Daeron rolled over, yawned and slowly opened his eyes, "Kidnapped you say; by whom?" He finally looked around at the sharp-toothed strangers and his eyes widened in recognition, "Oh, greetings Lady Eidothea. How fare the mermaids?"

"Well indeed, fair elf," replied Eidothea politely. She gestured to the two mermaids playing tug-of-war with Fendi, "Helena, Melitta, leave the poor halfman alone. You're scaring him. My apologies young one, they won't harm you. They've had more than their share of sailors today."

Halfling and fairy shuddered involuntarily.

She gave him an appraising stare. "I sense an important purpose about you, young Fendi. We will return you to the mainland as soon as the weather allows."

"Thank-you, my Lady," the halfling said earnestly.

Daeron swam across the water to the check on the others. "I think they'll be alright," he said to Fendi with a warning glance towards the sharp-toothed mermaids.

"Now, young halfman," Eidothea said to Fendi, "It will be a while before the storm eases, but then we can take you to land. Tell me about your journey here, I sense an adventure." The mermaids crowded around the apprehensive halfling who backed slowly away as he began to recount his tale:

"Well, my Lady, it was a strange series of events that led us to your underwater Coral City. It began back home in Southdale, far away in the South Lands. My friend Randir and I witnessed a group of Vergai soldiers coming through a portal. We overheard them say that they were going to steal the Elven Jewel from Lakehaven

and escape through another portal at Bamber's Brook, so we set off for Lakehaven by pony to warn the elves.

"We travelled as quickly as possible, but they were quicker. We were unable to prevent them stealing the jewel, so made for Bamber's Brook. Along the way our companions you see here: Sienna, a halfling huntress; Daeron; these two dwarfs; a Diagro knight and a mountain man joined our party. The Ancient Oracle showed us a vision which foretold the battle at Bamber's Brook and the search for a mage to find a way of defeating our enemy.

*"Unfortunately some of the Vergai had already escaped with the Elven Princess, who **is** the jewel, by the time we reached Bamber's Brook. Our army of dwarves, men and goblins defeated the Vergai in the Zanzi Grasslands and we destroyed the portal by killing the wizards who created it. We left two hundred dwarves there in case the portal reopens, and the others returned to Diamond City. The goblins and trolls departed also, saying they would happily play 'bash bash' with the Vergai again."*

Fendi paused and looked sorrowful before continuing, *"We stayed a day in Bamber's Brook to bury the dead and pay them tribute. My father, Old Fandri, was killed by the Vergai, and we have all suffered losses. Then our leader, Asher Grey, the dark-haired human yonder, led us to Port Lesslar and charted a ship to the Warrigal River and the Elven Forest. We've been at sea for three days now so I hope we'll make land soon, for we halflings and our bond fairies suffer terrible seasickness.*

The mermaids listened intently to Fendi's tale and now crowded around him again, stroking his arms and hair. The fearful halfling nervously said, "I thank-you again for your hospitality here, Lady Eidothea, but we would appreciate being on our way again as soon as possible, for the Vergai mean to overrun Reloria and destroy all that we love."

Despite the disappointed cries of the mermaids, Eidothea nodded her head. Fendi glanced at the many mermaids and asked, "Excuse me Lady Eidothea, but why there are no mermen?"

Laughter echoed strangely around the watery room. "No young halfling, there are no mermen. If we need a man we lure one from his ship. Those pirates you hired were the only men still brave enough to sail this sea."

A maroon-haired mermaid entered the cavern from below the water level, "My Lady, the storm is abating. Do you really wish us to take these walkers to Te Mātau?"

"Why yes, thank-you Myrrine," Lady Eidothea said, turning to Fendi. "We shall accompany you to your original destination. We'll make pressure bubbles for you to breathe on the journey to the surface."

As Daeron roused the others, Eidothea drew a circle in the air around the halfling's head with her golden sceptre. It felt as though he was wearing spherical helmet, and when he dipped his head into the water, the air came with him, allowing him to breathe easily. Holding Fendi-La tightly, they descended into the water and the maroon-haired mermaid held onto his arm, towing them through the water. Glancing behind, Fendi saw his companions were following with the mermaids' help.

It was a strange journey under the coral dome. They swam past many water plants, coral growth and brightly-coloured fish. One large open clam shell revealed dozens of tiny mermaid babies being fed small fish by an orange-haired mermaid. She smiled, sharp teeth glinting, and waved at the passing hunters.

Once they left the glowing dome, natural light filtered down from the surface above and the hunters were led slowly upwards. Dozens of mermaids followed behind them, and nervous fish scurried to get out of their path.

Nearby, Fendi saw the sunken Buccaneer lying on its side on the sea floor, small bubbles still trailed upward from the large gash in its hull.

*   *   *

"Fools' gold! We're stranded, shipwrecked in the middle of the ocean," moaned Baja. "What are those man-eating mermaids planning to do with us?"

The hunters had reached the surface of the Coral Sea and were beset by choppy waves, with no sign of a ship or land in sight.

It was Daeron who answered him, "Their leader, Eidothea has sensed some important purpose in young Fendi and granted him safe passage. She is a magical being who is given to having premonitions. Whilst she usually allows the mermaids free rein of any sailors cast overboard, she has offered us her protection. It seems to be a recurring theme that we are aided in our quest when we need it most." He finished speaking and looked thoughtful as they bobbed in the waves, now magically calmed by the Lady's sceptre.

Fendi introduced the hunters to Lady Eidothea. Instead of a bow, she made a huge leap out of the water and somersaulted through the air, splashing the surprised hunters. The halfling asked her, "My Lady, how much are you able to assist us in our quest? We must hasten to the Warrigal River and afterwards we need to continue on to the Sea of Orianth to delay the Vergai's battleships, waiting just beyond the elven shield to invade the West Lands. We can offer you some diamonds in payment and we would be grateful for any help you can offer us."

Lady Eidothea stroked her golden sceptre as she said, "Of course, young Fendi, the mermaids will ally with you for the chance to kill these Vergai. We will take you to Te Mātau on the Warrigal River and then go on to defend the west. May I see the diamonds please? I have a love of sparkly things."

Baja the dwarf reluctantly retrieved a small number of diamonds from the Elven Princess' jewellery box. Lady Eidothea's eyes glittered greedily at the sight of the sparkling jewels. Baja gave her a diamond set in a silver necklace in payment, though her hungry eyes reluctantly watched him close the small chest. The hunters however, were amazed, that despite the storm and loss of their weapons, Baja still held the chest tightly under his arm.

Asher clapped young Fendi on his back, "Well done lad," he said in his lilting voice. "You are a fine negotiator and the mermaids are a grand asset. They could help steer the Vergai ships off course or even break their hulls with the Lady's sceptre. Well done indeed."

The young halfling huntress, Sienna, also gave Fendi a pat on the back in congratulations. Blushing bright red, he turned away in embarrassment, for he was quite infatuated with the pretty huntress.

Meanwhile, Asher, Raja and Sir Varnon were lashing barrels together from the shipwreck. Several of the mermaids also brought a large piece of timber decking up from the wreck, which was fastened on the top to form a raft. Once finished, they climbed aboard and sat down, drying quickly in the warm afternoon.

"I miss my war hammer," complained Baja, as he rested his treasure chest and dragon's tooth dagger on the raft.

A watery hand tapped him on the shoulder and he turned to see their weapons and equipment rise slowly out of the water, followed by the sharp-toothed smiles of four mermaids, each of whom kissed Baja before disappearing beneath the waves.

A high-pitched whistle from Lady Eidothea attracted a pod of dolphins. She gave each a rope attached to the raft. With the aid of dolphins and mermaids, it sped across the waters of the Coral Sea, past dangerous reefs and coral outcrops toward Te Mātau and the Warrigal River.

The sun set pink across the far coastline, revealing a small moon and the twin planet of Zanarah, high in the sky overhead. It was currently in close orbit to Zumar and continents were easily discernible under swirling orange cloud formations. As Zanarah and the moon shed their silvery light in the growing darkness, the hunters huddled miserably on their raft.

*   *   *

Two days later, when the mermaids were guiding them between two islands, Daeron had a vision.

A reflection of his elven Princess, Shari-Rose was gazing intently into a hand-mirror. He knew from these visions that she was imprisoned in the Ar'gon Tower in the land of Vergash by the one-eyed giant, Emperor Chi'garu. The Cyclops ruler had destroyed her magical elven jewel with a burning beam of white-hot light from his eye, and was the irresistible force behind the Vergai invasion. They also knew he was now sending Vergai to invade the Eastern Outpost. This had been valuable intelligence for Daeron and his fellow hunters, in their quest to save the Princess and restore the elven shield.

Princess Shari-Rose was looking better than in Daeron's last vision. Her long red-blonde hair was neatly brushed out and she wore a clean white dress. She looked as though she had been eating well, instead of refusing her food, as she had done previously. Her cheeks had a rosy glow and there was a sparkle in her bright green eyes.

Daeron was puzzled for a second over why she looked so happy, and then he felt a wave of her magic. It started as a slight tingle and then it went all the way through his body. The Princess seemed to glow, and tiny sparkles surrounded her. The brown, lifeless crystal rose at the base of the Princesses' neck now began to shine with a burst of magical energy, as the Princess poured her power into it. A blast of rainbow colour reflected from the jewel, spilling outward towards the mirror, with some beams bouncing against the mirror and flowing back into the crystal. The colours flared very brightly for a moment and then suddenly disappeared. Daeron stared hopefully at the brown crystal, looking intently for some sign that it would be restored, and then, ... deep within the furled petals in the centre of the crystal, a barely perceptible rainbow light flickered. Shari-Rose saw it too, a wave of relief and hope washed over her and she jumped high in the air with glee.

Daeron caught a quick glance of her drab cell, with its giant-size bed and high window, before the vision faded and his consciousness returned to the raft.

He shared the news of his vision with his fellow hunters and they all felt as he did, that it was a sign that the elven crystal could be restored and again be a major factor in turning the tables on the Vergai. Daeron only wished that there were some way he could communicate with the lonely Princess to let her know how proud he was of her persistence, but for now at least, it seemed, she wouldn't know that her knowledge was shared with her loyal guardian.

*   *   *

The next day passed uneventfully. Mermaids and dolphins guided the raft swiftly through the dangerous coral straits, passing atolls and islands in the beautiful blue-green waters. The waves were smaller here and the halflings finally began to enjoy the voyage as their nausea abated, though the food that the mermaids brought them - fresh water, raw fish and seaweed - they had to force themselves to eat to keep up their strength.

However, the scenery was beautiful, with small islands, white beaches and swaying nut trees. Many of these islands were inhabited by the Vaimelie, a race of black-skinned fishermen, whose long boats trawled the blue-green waters. Some of the lithe Vaimelie women were seen diving for pearls as the men stood guard against predatory fish. It looked a simple, peaceful existence and Randir wished they could visit the islands.

The mermaids were intrigued that wherever the fairies were, they always managed to grow their toadstools at night to sleep upon. Three red and white spotted growths were attached to the deck of their wooden raft. Each night the fairies would dance and sing above these toadstools and their healing magic would renew the energies of the halflings. The food that the halflings' ate, sustained their fairies, as there was no nectar for them to drink.

On the third day since leaving Coral City, they reached the mouth of the mighty Warrigal River, which Raja explained was the biggest river in Reloria, beginning in the Great Elven Heart. As they passed a large island, hundreds of seabirds hovered in the air currents or swooped down to catch fish in the river.

Randir was eager to reach dry land after their long sea voyage. He saw Fendi and Sienna watching the scenery together, quite sombre these days, as both had lost their fathers recently. Sienna's father was killed several weeks ago by a bear in the Wild Woods, and Old Fandri had been slain during a Vergai attack.

Easy-going Randir knew that sharing their grief together was important, but he also tried hard to lighten their spirits. In his usual clumsy way, he skidded on the wet deck, catching hold of Fendi just before both toppled overboard into the clear blue river. The halflings and fairies all laughed at his awkwardness, while large blue dolphins nudged them both back toward the raft.

Randir was pleased to see his friends smile and joined in their laughter while the fairies danced around them, tinkling the golden bells atop their caps.

The hunters peered eagerly along the banks of the wide river, eventually spotting the small village of Te Mātau hugging the northern banks. The landscape on both sides of the river was thick jungle and the halflings caught occasional glimpses of large primates in the forest to the south. Randir suspected the jungle to the north would be nigh impassable and that all trade probably came by the river.

Gazing into the river depths, Raja glimpsed a spotted form as long as several ships undulating beneath them, and suddenly a wail rang out from the mermaids towing the raft. The river thrashed and the companions saw an orange-haired mermaid held aloft by an enormous snake.

"River-snake!" cried Raja, as the green and brown serpent wrapped its coils around her. The snake's huge mouth stretched over her dripping head, preparing to swallow the unfortunate mermaid.

Lady Eidothea cried out in rage and a blast of water erupted from her sceptre, causing the deadly snake to hiss and drop the mermaid into the water where she was quickly pulled to safety.

A large whirlpool appeared and the hunters watched the snake swirling round the maelstrom. Angry

Eidothea raised the golden sceptre, lifting the snake and several hundred gallons of water high into the air. While the water splashed back into the river, the snake was tossed into the canopy of the jungle with a flick of her wrist. Trees groaned under the weight of the giant reptile and branches snapped off as the snake fell back into the river, flicked its long tail and vanished upriver.

Eidothea swam over to the raft and said to Asher, "Unfortunately we cannot go any farther upriver, but we will honour our pact and await the Vergai in the Sea of Orianth." She wrapped her arm protectively around the orange mermaid and said goodbye.

With a swishing of tails, the colourful creatures undulated through the waters and were soon heading around the island and out to sea. One maroon-haired lass blew a kiss to Randir as the hunters thanked and farewelled the mermaids and dolphins.

"Well, today is turning out to be full of surprises," declared Baja, and as if on cue, the heavens opened. One minute, the air was heavy with moisture and the next, torrential rain. The companions in the raft could barely see each other, let alone the village on the far shore. Heavy drops of water thumped against their skin and the raft started to sink.

"Quickly Daeron!" yelled Asher, "Let's get out of here!" The man and elf grabbed wooden planks, paddling with superhuman speed until the raft bumped against a pylon jutting out of the water. Underneath the suspended village of Te Mātau, they tied their raft next to several intricately carved wooden boats.

CHAPTER 3: JUNGLE TREK

The jungle along the Warrigal River was so dense that the villagers built platforms out along the water. The companions climbed a wooden ladder hanging from the floor above. They emerged at one end of a long enclosed building. The roof was supported by a large tree-trunk beam suspended by y-shaped logs at either end. The thatched palm fronds kept out the heavy rain. The walls were made of wood painted in blue, black and white, with intricate carvings everywhere the hunters looked; many featured grimacing faces with protruding tongues while others featured swirling patterns of waves and dots.

At the far end of the building a group of elders sat in a circle. A grey-headed man stood and slowly walked towards them, followed by the others who encircled the hunters.

Old grey-hair held up a hand in greeting.

"Hello. We are the Mātau people and I am Amiri," he said. "Welcome to our village." The hunters gazed with interest at the elders, all of whom were solidly-built and very fit for their age, though the dotted black tattoos on their faces made them look quite frightening.

Motioning Fendi to accompany him, Asher approached with palms open. "Greetings to you Amiri, and your fellow Mātau, I am Asher Grey of Flame Mountain and these be my companions. We come on an urgent quest because Reloria has been invaded and we must hasten to the desert outpost north of here. We need to hire a guide if you can help us." Then Asher quickly outlined their journey.

Amiri stepped forward until he was right in front of Asher and bent his face to Asher's until their foreheads touched. He went to each member of the group in this way and they introduced themselves. Looking a little surprised to hear where each had come from, he paused thoughtfully when the introductions had been made.

The elder rubbed his chin with his thumb and forefinger and spoke, "You are an unusual group of hunters to be sure. I'd be surprised if you have any gold left after travelling with Captain Halldor and his band of pirates. We can lead you on a path to the north and from there you will find others who can guide you. You are welcome to dine with us tonight and leave with our guide in the morning."

Amiri gestured to a large rack of wooden and bone weapons of many designs. Although they looked both sharp and strong, they were also beautiful in their curving forms and intricate carving. It appeared the Mātau were both warriors and artisans. Sienna went over to the rack and handled some of the weapons with admiration.

"We are a proud people, young huntress, and we defend our territory," said Amiri. "We have enemies both upriver and in the islands trying to claim our village. Also pirates sail up and down the east coast robbing any ship or village they see. We can defend ourselves." The elder picked up a long wooden spear and expertly twirled it round his head. He grimaced and showed the whites of his eyes as he stood in a threatening pose. Alarmed, the hunters stepped backward away from the scary figure.

"Don't worry, young ones," old Amiri said, looking cheerful once again. If we hadn't trusted you, you'd have been floating in the river before we had said hello. We will feed you and send you on your way tomorrow. The rain will cease in an hour."

"Thank-you Amiri," said Asher politely. "We really appreciate your hospitality."

Reassured, the hunters relaxed, watching the Mātau working together to prepare their meal. They were shown around the village of many long buildings, half of which jutted out over the river. One was a kitchen, with the food being buried under the fire's coals to cook. Randir, Fendi and Sienna stayed to watch, for their tummies rumbled from the hard biscuit and salted meat aboard the ship, followed by the almost unpalatable raw fish and seaweed.

Randir in particular watched the cooking with great interest, for the fish and purple root cakes were cooked with hot stones underground. He happily chatted about food to the young ladies gathered around the fire pit, but the brown-skinned women were interested in the halfling's village and adventures in the South Lands. His fairy Randir-La also was the source of great interest to the villagers, particularly when she obliged by giving an impromptu dance with Fendi-La and the male fairy, Sienna-Li. The fairies' golden bells tinkled as their green clothes whirled in a blur near the high wooden beams.

Fendi and Sienna stood a little distance away, watching the teeming rain through a hooded window. Fendi carefully placed his arm around the young huntress and when she didn't move, he pulled her close. He could feel the warmth from her body, smell her sweet scent and he stroked her long brown hair, tied back in a tangled ponytail.

Sienna gave a relaxed sigh and turned towards Fendi. "I'm so glad that I am here with you Fendi and sharing this quest. There have been some terrible days and some good ones, but being with you has made everything special to me." She shrugged off her long bow to the dirt floor and held onto Fendi's strong arms. "My father taught me to be independent from an early age, but now I feel a need for comfort and companionship."

Fendi held his breath as she stroked her fingers gently along his cheeks. His face was slowly losing the pimply covering and a patchy beard now grew on his chin. He could feel the rough calluses on her fingers from years of hunting with the long bow, as she gently ran her fingers over his lips, which trembled and parted at her touch. Sienna leaned forward and gave him a slow, deep kiss. At first Fendi was stunned with wonder, but he quickly responded with a long kiss in return, feeling the softness of her generous lips.

It was as though Randir and the Mātau did not exist, for the two young halflings were lost in the moment.

Sienna's fingers played with the wavy brown hair at the back of Fendi's neck and he gently ran his hands down her back. After a long, lingering embrace, they finally came up for air only to realise that the others in the room had all gone silent.

They slowly turned to see a dozen eyes quietly watching them. Randir broke the silence with a friendly chuckle and the young ladies tittered among themselves. Fendi blushing a deep red, stepped back from Sienna, until only their hands were touching. Randir gave him an approving nod, before turning back to wrap an arm around two Mātau maidens, resuming their lively conversations.

Fendi felt rather shy and awkward, but clung tightly to Sienna's hand, both seemingly intent on watching the rain in silence. He wondered what she was thinking, but was too embarrassed to ask and afraid of spoiling the moment. Sienna too seemed unsure of what to do next, for she had only lived with her father and was inexperienced with company.

They stood at the window watching the rain for a long while, until it stopped as abruptly as it had begun.

*   *   *

The meal of cooked fish and potato cakes seemed like a feast to the hungry travellers. Almost a hundred villagers had come to share in the meal, each bringing food with them. There was also a substantial fruit platter for desert and the hunters enjoyed the rainforest flavours. The juicy yellow juju was their favourite and Randir kept some for the next day's trek.

A small furry creature with a long curled tail brazenly came to share Randir's food. The halfling was a little concerned to see its long claws and sharp teeth, but Amiri said she was a furmal and, although still wild, would not harm him unless provoked. Randir gave the grey furmal a gentle pat on the back and it hopped up onto his shoulder, gnawing on a juju seed gripped tightly in her little paws.

Raja asked many questions of the Mātau people about their village and culture.   He was fascinated by how they made their clothes from mulber tree bark and flax from the far side of the river. The men wore a belted skirt and their bare chests showed off their tattoos. The ladies and girls wore the skirt with a sleeveless top which had colourful, geometric patterns woven into the material.   The elders' light and colourful feathered cloaks were all they needed in the tropical heat.

Sir Varnon now sat beside the mountain man and the dwarves, looking quite at home on the woven mats in the tropical rainforest. Baja however, was disappointed at the lack of ale, but happily chatted to the villagers. He hadn't succeeded in forming a card game, but was not giving up hope.

 Sir Varnon was scraping rust from his metal breastplate after the long sea voyage.

As the fire died down, Asher's yellow-green eyes gave off a slight glow as he pondered their journey ahead.

"Where would we be finding a wizard to join our quest?" he asked of Raja.

The knowledgeable dwarf sighed deeply and replied, "The Ancient Oracle said to seek out a mage, not a wizard. A mage is a wizard of Nnanell with three or more powers, though I doubt there's one to be found anywhere in Reloria."

Asher smiled back at him and there was hope in his lilting voice as he exclaimed, "They've not been wrong as yet. Look at you, Varnon, a dragon-killing knight who came to us on the Oracle's request. They were right then, so we must have faith that this will come to pass."

*   *   *

The day dawned hot and steamy. Randir awoke with a start to find something warm and furry across his eyes. He yelped and leapt up, just as the grey furmal scratched his arm and jumped to the floor, equally startled.

Randir regretted alarming the little creature and tried to tempt it back with the whole juju fruit lying next to his bedroll. "Here you go little furmal. I'm sorry. Come and have some of this tasty juju." He offered her the fruit which she grasped with tiny front paws, tore a strip off and rolled the rest along the ground towards Randir's feet. The halfling gave a surprised laugh and bent to share the fruit with her.

"You seem to have made a furry friend," said a friendly female voice. Randir looked up to see a tall woman with flowing black hair standing in front of him. Her face was pretty on one side, but the other half was marred by a scar which ran from her forehead to her jaw, right through a vacant eye socket.

She looked kindly at him and spoke again, "I am Rere, your guide to the Village of the Sacred Shrine. Asher and I have agreed to leave early, for we have a long way to walk. I think that you have made a little friend there with Kulana. She may follow you on our travels."

Randir patted the furmal's soft back, running his hand along her long dark tail which curled at the end. "Kulana is such a pretty name for her," he said, as he held his hand out, she ran nimbly up his arm to perch on his shoulder. He could feel her claws holding on through his shirt, but they were not uncomfortable enough for him to shift her. "She can come with me if she wants to. She's such a cute little thing," he added.

"I don't mind," Rere said, "as long as you let her return with me when you near the desert. She wouldn't survive the heat and winds there."

"Alright," agreed Randir, "you can bring her back. It would be nice to have something to pat on the journey." He gave a knowing look at Fendi, who turned bright red and looked out the window. Both their fairies giggled in amusement, bouncing up and down on their toadstool beds.

Sienna was nowhere to be seen and Randir guessed they were being shy and awkward again after their kiss yesterday. He gave an inward sigh, resolving to give Fendi some helpful advice when they had some time alone together. His friend seemed quite naive, despite growing up with a sister and several girls his age in the village.

Rere began the trek just after daybreak. The hunters travelled fairly light, just bedrolls, weapons and food. Randir walked with their Mātau guide in the lead, while the furmal alternated between perching on his shoulder and scampering along the track beside him.

Next came Baja and Raja, who seemed to have woken up grumpy. They were exchanging heated words and bumping shoulders as they walked the narrow path through the rainforest. Following were Asher and Sir Varnon, who had made an unlikely friendship after an awkward beginning, when the knight Prince had ordered the mountain man to be taken to the stocks. They had settled their differences over a duel and now admired and respected each other. The same couldn't be said for the majority of the other knights who had continued to spit at Asher's boots until he led them to victory at Bamber's Brook. Both men hoped that this victory would start to dissipate the generations of hate between their races.

Bringing up the rear were the other two halflings and Daeron the elf. Fendi and Sienna walked near to each other, but avoided each other's gaze. By contrast, their fairies held hands and flew happily between the obstinate pair. Fendi feigned a keen interest in the men's conversation and Sienna was collecting branches to make into arrows as they walked along. She did glance at Fendi several times and he at her, but still unsure of each other's feelings, they were careful to avoid eye contact.

Daeron was keenly aware of every rustle and crunch. The woods teemed with life: the flocks of squawking screechers, small hoppers and wild hounds that slunk through the underbrush. The bird life too was prolific with colours of all hues, including a long blue-necked bird that peered at them through the trees, before darting away on equally long legs.

Rere led them north from the river village, deep into the rainforest, keeping a brisk pace despite the oppressive humidity and boggy mud. There were large primates in the forest, in extensive family groups, seemingly disinterested in the hunters passing close to them. An orange-haired ape grooming its infant's hair brought a wistful smile to Fendi's face as he remembered his mother grooming his hair, far away in Southdale and he felt a twinge of homesickness.

Baja also saw them and turned to his brother. "We could leave you here to play with the apes, Raja. You look like one of them."

Too busy laughing, Baja failed to see the hairy dwarven fist that laid him flat on the ground. The usually quiet Raja laughed loudly as he extended his hand to help up his brother, but Baja grabbed hold of the double-headed axe which protruded over Raja's shoulder and gave the dwarf a light tap on the head with it. Raja collapsed to the ground, but it was only a ruse. He dragged his brother down and laughing, the two of them rolled and wrestled in the mud, their companions watching on in amusement.

Eventually Baja conceded, "No more, please no more," while their audience burst into laughter at the muddy sight.

"You might want to check yourselves for leeches," Asher remarked with a sly smile and the two dwarves scampered back down the path, pulling off clothes as they ran. "Don't take too long," Ash called after them, "we be in a hurry to beat these Vergai."

"Do you think there are leeches around here?" asked Fendi.

"Not really, but it's fun to watch," replied the mountain man in his lilting voice and the companions to burst into laughter once more. The fairies joined in with bells jingling.

* * *

They travelled quickly through the steamy jungle, but by mid-afternoon the heavens opened once more, saturating the travellers. Rere led them to an unusually large tree with dozens of thin intertwining trunks making a cave-like hollow underneath.

Raja played a soothing tune on his pan pipes as they huddled together, waiting for the rain to ease. Rere seemed unconcerned by the dripping water though the companions wriggled to try and find a dry space, while Randir and Fendi swatted insects buzzing round their heads.

"I'm not happy with these steamy summers," said an exasperated Randir as he smacked a large stingeler which had bitten him through his trousers.

"Well, actually, this is nearly the start of our winter, because you have just crossed the equator," remarked Rere. "Not that there's much difference in our seasons, except during the monsoon season when we have cyclonic winds."

Randir looked at Sir Varnon in disbelief and the knight nodded, "Yes young halfling, I am afraid she is right. But look on the bright side; it will cool as we go north. We are heading towards the desert where it is much drier."

Rere agreed, "Yes. But first we pass through the swamps to reach the Village of the Secret Shrine. From there the rainforest turns into a drier stringbark forest before petering out into the desert. It will be winter in a few days though, when the desert nights get very cold. There are such extremes in this part of Reloria. I don't know which is better: hot and steamy by day or dry and freezing at night."

"Well there's a cheery thought," muttered Baja glumly. "I don't suppose there'll be anything decent to eat or drink for the next couple of weeks. I do miss my barrel of ale."

"Cheer up brother," said Raja. "At least you don't have the Elven Jewel bossing you around. Can you imagine the grief she is giving her captors? I think they'll be glad when we come to rescue her."

"They won't live long enough to be glad about anything," muttered Daeron darkly. The white-haired elf had an angry look in his pale blue eyes as he spoke. "The Ar'gon Tower will lie in rubble on the lands of Vergash when I am through with them." He angrily lashed out with his sword, slicing cleanly through a branch. There hadn't been any visions of Princess Shari-Rose for a few days and he anxiously wondered if she was alright.

Randir sat next to Rere under the large tree. Ignoring the steady dripping of water down his neck, he patted Kulana while studying the Mātau woman's face out of the corner of his eye. The long pale scar down her brown cheek looked old, as though it had happened many years ago. Her one good eye was large and round and beautiful, tattoos extended from her temple down to her chin and she wore a headband to keep her dripping black hair from her eyes.

Unable to help himself, Randir asked her about the scar. Looking angry, she replied, "It was from a pirate attack when I was ten years old. They raided our village and killed several of my people. The Captain took my eye as a reminder that the pirates ruled the waters. Now there is a bounty on Captain Halldor's head and he no longer sails the Warrigal River." Her eye flashed heatedly in the dripping hollow.

Asher replied, "Then you'll be pleased to know that what remains of Captain Halldor lies beneath the Coral Sea. The Buccaneer capsized in a storm and the mermaids made sure that none of the pirates survived. Those mermaids have no love of the pirates."

"Of that, I am certain," said the Mātau woman. "We hear many stories of the mermaids causing the pirates to wreck their ships, or throw themselves overboard. Good riddance to the scoundrels; I have no sympathy for the murderous villains. I only wish that I'd had a chance to kill him myself."

The companions waited until the rain abruptly stopped before emerging from the hollow tree. The clouds had blown over and the sky once more was blue. Zanarah and its moon were visible in the western sky, and the planet glowed orange, which Fendi found strangely fascinating.

*   *   *

A whole week passed in much the same fashion. Rere lead the companions through the lush rainforest, showing them what native foods to eat. They caught birds and small animals, roasting them on fires each evening, and while it rained in the afternoon, the rainfall lessened each day, for which the companions were grateful.

The rainforest finally gave way to a tall drier forest. Rere pointed out the different kinds of trees to the halflings and Raja. As they walked along they were shown red trunks, paper-bark, ash-bark and stringbark trees. Occasionally Rere pointed out bushy-tailed furmals sleeping high in the branches, or sometimes snakes and long-eared hoppers hiding along their trail.

The path their guide took was marked by small piles of stones next to trees where the path divided. Randir noticed the tree trunks next to the stones bore writing which he could not read, but presumed that it indicated the correct direction.

CHAPTER 4: VILLAGE OF THE SACRED SHRINE

On the seventh day since leaving the river, Randir was woken suddenly by an orange snake slithering over his legs. A low voice beside him whispered, "Keep very still. That's a deadly Zumari snake and he can kill you instantly." Randir recognised Rere's voice and froze immediately. He couldn't see his little furmal, Kulana, but hoped she was somewhere safe.

The snake licked the air with its forked tongue before gliding away. Sighing with relief, Randir sprang to his feet. He spied Randir-La up a nearby tree with Kulana and ran towards them, tripping over sleeping Sienna in his haste. Her brown hair was spread out like a fan around her beautiful face and Sienna-Li slept beside her on his toadstool.

She woke with a start as Randir came crashing down on top of her. "Randir, what are you doing? Get off me, you big lump!" She pushed him off, but Randir grabbed her arm and sat there shaking. Seeing the fear in his eyes, Sienna's annoyance changed to concern. "Randir, are you alright?" she asked.

"No," he said nervously, "I was almost bitten by a deadly Zumari snake. I could have died!"

Sienna gave him a big, comforting hug and said with a smile, "It's all right, Randir. You're safe here with me." She patted his hair and held him until he calmed down. Regaining his composure, Randir thanked her and went to greet Kulana and Randir-La as they came down from the tree. Sienna smiled at the clumsy halfling, but missed the look of jealousy that crossed Fendi's face.

The commotion woke the remaining hunters and they were soon on their way.

Sienna-Li was in a cheeky mood and tried to ride on Kulana's back as the little furmal scampered after Randir, climbing up trees, jumping from branch to branch with the little fairy clinging tightly to her tail. At length, tiring of the game, the furmal swung upside-down to shake off the irritating little fairy, who chuckled with glee, and flapping his iridescent wings he flitted off to join a group of bright blue butterflies.

Randir scolded him good-naturedly and hurried after the other companions further down the forest trail.

Fendi was waiting for him by a tree. The others disappeared around a bend.

"Thanks for waiting Fendi," Randir said, giving Fendi a pat on the shoulder. He started off down the path, but stopped when he realised that Fendi hadn't moved. "What's the matter?" he asked.

Fendi clenched his fist, his face red as he spoke slowly between clenched teeth, "You know exactly what the matter is, don't you? The only girl I like, who ever liked me back and you have to go and steal her from me. How could you?" His arms were tense against his sides as he struggled to control himself.

Randir was shocked by this. "Fendi, I don't know what you think happened," he said, "but there is nothing between Sienna and me. I think of her as a sister, nothing more."

"But I saw you two embrace, just now, while she was only wearing her underclothes," Fendi said uncertainly.

"Oh Fendi," laughed Randir. "I was scared by a deadly snake and tripped over my own feet trying to run away. I fell on top of her while she was asleep and probably scared her half to death too. She was just trying to reassure me and kindly didn't tell me how daft I was. She's a lovely girl and you should tell her how you feel."

"Do you think she might actually like me?" asked Fendi dubiously.

"Oh course she does, silly. I saw you two kissing back at the village. She definitely likes you, but doesn't know how to show it either. Just go and talk to her and hold her hand. I'm sure you can figure it out together." Randir gave a sigh and shook his head. He didn't know how Fendi could negotiate treaties between sworn enemies and still not be able to talk to a girl he clearly loved.

"Come on Randir, we're losing sight of them," called his fairy, and the two halflings ran to catch up with their companions. Chasing their fairies through the trees they emerged in a clearing, skidding to a halt at what they saw.

Their companions were surrounded by Centaurs, half-man, half-horse, armed with bronze tridents that pointed menacingly at the hunters. Asher and Sir Varnon had dropped their weapons on the ground and the others were in the process of doing so, raising flat-palmed hands in a gesture of surrender. A brown-haired centaur stepped up behind the stunned halflings and nudged them into the circle with their friends.

To the hunters' surprise, the centaurs then all looked expectantly to the sky with their tridents raised. The sun was just visible over the tall trees beside the planet Zanarah. As the crowd of hunters and centaurs watched, the twin planet slowly edged across in front of the sun and darkness spread over the land.

A deep voice boomed out in the silence, "It is written in the stars that the saviours of Reloria will appear in the Sacred Shrine at this Winter Conjunction. You are the hunters of legend who it is said will restore peace to our lands now under threat of invasion." The hunters turned as one to see a large centaur pacing regally towards them. His black horse's body looked strong and muscular and black hair flowed behind him like a mane.

"Welcome, hunters of Reloria. I am Alpheratz, King of the Centaurs. Who among you is the leader?"

Asher stepped forward, "I am Asher Grey of Flame Mountain." He gestured to each of the companions as he introduced them, "Sir Varnon, Prince of the Diagro Plains; Daeron, of the elves; Baja and Raja of Diamond City; Huntress Sienna of the Wild Woods; and Randir and Fendi of the Southdale halflings with their fairies. This is our guide, Rere of the Mātau people, who has brought us thus far. We come in peace and seek your aid in travelling to the desert outpost to battle the Vergai invaders."

At a small gesture from their King, the centaurs lowered their tridents and silently watched the orange planet conclude its eclipse of the sun. The hunters remained wary of the centaurs, but as the creatures withdrew, they cautiously collected their weapons from the ground. Randir noticed a trembling Rere trying to hide behind a tree. He hurried over to her and whispered with concern, "Are you alright?"

The Mātau woman shook her head and whispered back, "These creatures make human sacrifices. This is as far as I will go with you. Good luck on your quest."

The tall halfling shook her hand in thanks and gave Kulana a hug. "I'm going to miss you, my cute little furmal," he said, handing the little creature back to Rere and watched its bushy brown tail curl around her neck. The furmal's big brown eyes seemed a little sad too, as she and Rere disappeared into the trees. Randir waved a silent goodbye.

Asher and Fendi meanwhile were speaking quietly with the centaurs. Alpheratz was looking quite disgusted at something they said and Randir went closer to listen.

The centaur King was angrily saying, "...may oblige you by riding on our backs, but will not stoop to wearing saddles like a common horse." The King raised his proud hawked nose and looked again at the sky. He appeared thoughtful for a moment, then slowly turned back to the companions. "Yes, it is written in the stars. We are to take you as far as the desert castle and from there you will find your own way. Come, we will prepare a feast to celebrate your arrival."

The centaur King led them towards a massive stone pyramid rising to many times the height of the forest. As they drew closer they saw weathered hieroglyphs both triangular and circular in form.

A stone bridge crossed the dry moat surrounding the edifice, and beyond a broad ramp spiralled up to the apex. There a long cylindrical object on a platform reflected a blinding light when the sun emerged from behind Zanarah.

"This is the Sacred Shrine," declared Apheratz reverently. He and the rest of the centaurs knelt at the base of the huge pyramid, but did not ascend the massive structure.

The land here was strewn with large flat rocks and a nearby cliff-face showed the quarry where they were sourced. Made of four upright standing stones with a flat roof overhead, the village huts were built in an arcing formation with two larger buildings set apart from the others. All were unfurnished, except for a large mound of cut leaf fronds on the dirt, and an open aqueduct brought water from the hills to the west.

Armed centaurs surrounded the hunters once again as more trotted out of the stone huts, including many beautiful females and juveniles. Fendi wondered if they were called mares and foals or women and children, but he was too intimidated to ask. Most of the female centaurs had a chest covering of long grasses woven together. Some of them were bare-chested and Fendi flushed bright red with embarrassment though the centaurs seemed oblivious to their lack of modesty. He tried hard not to look or think about them, and turned his attention to Sienna instead, but she gazed at him with an amused expression.

Flustered, he feigned a great interest in the dirt around his feet.

Randir was excited at the thought of the promised feast. He could smell interesting aromas coming from the cook fires and wondered what the centaurs had in store for them, for the week-long trek had left him with a very large appetite. Sienna was skilled at hunting hoppers, but Randir hadn't cared much for their gamey taste.

Rere too had offered alternative foods including potatoes, nuts, small reptiles and forest plants. The Mātau woman had been quite skilled at cooking these over a campfire, but they had not been to Randir's liking either. Crossing his stubby fingers, he hoped the centaurs planned some tastier morsels today.

While the food was being prepared, King Alpheratz introduced several of the centaurs; among them a red-haired centaur named Fornax who seemed rather grumpy for no obvious reason, and Saiph who had brown hair with a thick white streak starting at his left temple. The last to be introduced was the seer, Carina, with blonde locks and coat, who seemed quite vague and mystical.

Randir's stomach was now rumbling loudly for he was desperately hungry. Unable to stand it any longer, he begged for something to eat.

The red-haired Fornax, who seemed to have taken a disliking to the hunters, replied rudely, "We do not eat during the daylight hours, for this dishonours the Gods."

Practically crying with frustration, Randir excused himself from the gathering to look for something to nibble. He was certain that he could not wait another four hours, no matter how good the food was going to be. He and his fairy wandered past the stone huts and found an orchard of fruit trees. His heart beat quickly as he walked among the trees of foreign fruits, not knowing what they were. He finally spied a loongafruit tree, and checking that no-one was looking, helped himself to two loongas.

As he sat beside the clump of trees enjoying the fruit, a young female centaur with flowing black hair and a white star on her torso wandered over to him. Not yet fully grown, her breast not yet developed, she looked at him with big brown eyes and smiled cheekily.

"I think it's a silly law too; not eating during the day, I mean. My dame says I'm going through a growth spurt because I'm hungry all the time," she said.

"Me too," Randir replied. "Hi, my name is Randir from the Southdale and this is my bond fairy, Randir-La. We go everywhere together. What's your name?"

"I'm Yildun. It means 'star' in Centauri." She gestured shyly to the white star on her black torso. "Have you been inside the pyramid?"

"No," Randir replied. "King Alpheratz said it was sacred so I don't suppose he will allow us to look. How do you get inside it?"

"There's a secret door half-way up. Why don't I wait for you at the bridge at midnight and we can sneak in together? Do you think the other halflings might like to see it too?"

"I'll ask them later. Thank-you, Yildun. I'd better get back to the elders before they realise I've been eating during the day. I'll see you tonight." They left the orchard by different paths, and then he caught up with Fendi in the village.

"Fendi, I think we have a little exploring to do tonight. Don't tell anyone but meet me at the moat bridge at midnight," Randir whispered.

"This is a bad idea," said Randir-La and Fendi-La nodded in agreement. "We'll be in big trouble if we're caught." Randir-La was never afraid to give the teenagers a piece of her mind.

But boys being boys, they were more interested in adventures rather than the wisdom of their bond fairies. Randir shook his head, "Not this time, fairy. We'll be as quiet as mice."

Fendi nodded conspiratorially, wise enough not to ask questions, yet always keen for adventures with Randir.

* * *

By the time dusk arrived, the food was further delayed by a concert performed for the visitors on a raised platform near the village. A group of male centaurs sang a chanting song in traditional Centauri. Their voices soared in complex harmonies, the beautiful sound bringing tears to the eyes of their audience.

Finally, the famished hunters sat around a large fire pit encircled by tiered stone benches, wide enough to accommodate the centaurs' long horse bodies.

Randir sighed happily when food was brought from the kitchen huts, but he and his companions were totally unimpressed by what they saw. Rather than the hoped-for meat and cooked vegetables, the platters contained giant white grubs in red sauce, crickets and enormous beetles on a bed of mixed green leaves. Randir shook his head, hoping the next dish would be edible. His companions stared in dismay at the centaurs hungrily devouring small insects in their hundreds, though Daeron, a vegetarian, ate the leafy garnishes. Randir plucked up the courage to ask the dark centaur beside him if there was any other meat.

"Do you mean mammals?" the centaur replied in a shocked voice. "Surely sentient creatures like you do not eat mammals! How barbaric!" The centaurs all fell silent at his raised voice.

King Alpharetz replied, "I have heard tales of men who eat large mammals and would hope that you hunters would be more discerning. What will you eat next? Centaurs?"

There was an awkward moment when everyone stared in shock at the hunters. Then a centaur laughed out loud. The others joined in the laughter, breaking the tension and it was obvious the creatures could not believe their guests could be so barbaric. Wisely the hunters joined in, chuckling to hide their guilt.

Randir looked at Fendi, watching his friend eat one of the large grubs covered in red sauce, gagging as he swallowed the insect whole. Fendi-La also looked rather faint and fluttered to the ground as though in a shock. Yet Randir thought it best not to offend the centaurs so took one himself. The skin was crispy as he bit it in half, the inside tasting of nuts. Swallowing it as quickly as possible, he took a large drink of water to make sure it had gone down. All-in-all it wasn't too bad, he thought, but the feast was not at all what he expected.

Fried spiders were next, unanimously declined by the hunters who watched in bewilderment as the centaurs clearly enjoyed these hairy-legged treats, which oozed fluid when bitten. Baked reptiles served in their skin followed, before the meal thankfully improved when large fruit platters appeared.

The feast concluded with a large cauldron of dark brown liquid, which Randir eyed this with suspicion, but the aroma was enticing and he accepted a cup. Intrigued by the sweet flavour, he eagerly welcomed a second helping when it was offered.

"What is this delicious drink?" he asked King Alpheratz. The dark-haired ruler smiled and told him that the drink was called caco and originally came from the jungle near the river. The trees were now cultivated in the centaurs' orchard and the drinks were sweetened with honey. "That's the most wonderful thing I've ever tasted," Randir declared earnestly. He asked for a third cup, but before he got to taste it, the three fairies drained the caco with reed straws.

The meal was followed by dancing and singing from the centaurs. The hunters were escorted to the dance floor and twirled round in ecstasy with the centaurs, for the caco had made them feel both calm and happy. The dwarves proved to be proficient dancers and taught Sienna some of their steps as they whirled her round. The young huntress smiled with elation, spinning so quickly Baja had to steady her.

Fendi half-heartedly partnered the young centaur, Yildun, at the edge of the floor, but only had eyes for Sienna, wishing he had the courage to dance with her himself.

The dancers finally collapsed into leafy beds, falling into a deep sleep.

* * *

"Randir, Randir, wake up!" whispered a voice in his ear. "It's midnight and we're going to the pyramid."

Randir was wakened by Fendi shaking his arm and the silhouette of Sienna framed in the doorway. After a few seconds he remembered they were due to meet Yildun at the pyramid and jumped to his feet. Naturally, being Randir, he tripped and only Fendi's strong arm kept him from falling onto the slumbering elf next to him. Dressing hurriedly, Randir met the other halflings outside the stone hut.

The outline of the pyramid was clearly defined in the bright moonlight. The campfire in the arena was now just glowing coals as they quietly scurried past, occasionally glimpsing families of centaurs sleeping in their huts. But as they neared the base of the shrine, a dark figure detached itself from the shadows.

Yildun nodded her head in silent greeting, her hooves barely making a sound as she led the halflings over the moat and up the ramp that wound its way up the pyramid. It was deceptively steep and the halflings' legs were aching by the time they reached the hidden doorway.

The young centaur's dark hair hid her face as she searched the stone for a hidden lever. Then a low whirring was heard inside the pyramid. The door slid back and Yildun reached inside for a flint and wooden torch. Lighting the torch she hurried them inside before they could be discovered. At a touch of another lever, the door swung back behind them and Yildun placed the torch in a holder in the centre of the room. The halflings and fairies gasped in wonder, for the flickering light was reflected in dozens of mirrors placed strategically around the walls, making the room almost as bright as day.

The pyramid was hollow and they stood on a small platform suspended in the centre of the enormous space. Looking down, they could not see how the platform was held up nor the floor of the chamber. The internal stone walls featured diagrams of star signs and mathematical equations, while in front of them the metal arms of a machine extended to various points around the inside of the pyramid.

"What is this place?" asked Fendi in amazement.

Yildun gave a nod of appreciation. "Magnificent, isn't it? It's a space observatory designed by the desert gnomes. There's a telescope on top of the pyramid which makes planets and stars appear closer when you look through it. In here we study the constellations and predict the future, for many of the wise centaurs dedicate their lives to research.

"Our ancestors foretold your coming many generations ago and we plan to ally with you for the coming war. Here, I will show you how the Centauri constellation is aligned right now." The young centaur stepped carefully over to the machine and adjusted several levers and cogs. The machine made a low grating noise, one of the large stone blocks moved aside in the pyramid's eastern wall, and they gazed awestruck at the constellation of Centauri through the window.

"It's amazing the centaurs can predict the exact placement of the stars, for they are constantly in motion," Sienna said. "Also, how do the elders know we are going to war together? Even we didn't know that."

"The centaurs have studied the stars for millennia," Yildun explained, "so they know the meanings of astrological events. Do you see the star in the constellation's eye? Well, it turned red yesterday just as our forefathers predicted. Centaur villages spread all across these lands are preparing to join with you into battle."

Yildun sighed, her long black hair falling across her face.

"What's wrong?" asked Randir with concern.

"I'm too young to go," Yildun said sadly. "My two big brothers have been training with the trident for years but they only let me watch. I wish I could go with you."

Randir gave her a brotherly hug. She reminded him of his younger siblings back home and he remembered their frustration at missing out on something exciting.

"Yildun, in thanks for showing us your sacred shrine, I present you with this friendship bracelet from the South Lands." He untied one of the several leather bracelets from his wrist he'd received from Southdale girls over the years. He tied it around her slender wrist, gratified by her expression of pride at helping the halflings.

Yildun grasped his hand tightly and pulled him over to the machine. "Come, we must leave before we are caught, but I have something else to show you." Turning a large wheel, she returned the cogs and levers to their original position, then led the halflings over to the stone door and pulled another lever. The low whirring noise re-occurred as they walked through and the door closed behind them.

They stealthily made their way to the small platform on top of the pyramid and Randir envied the fairies, who flew up the steep ramp and perched on the long cylinder to wait for them.

Pausing for a moment, the centaur gestured down to the sleeping village, explaining to her companions that the huts were set out to map the constellations of Centauri, Eridanus and Perseus.

The platform itself was barely large enough for Yildun's long horse body, but she adjusted the telescope and gestured for them to come and look. One by one, the halflings gasped in surprise as they looked through the small glass eyepiece. An orange and brown planet filled the entire view through the cylinder, the magnification so great, clouds could be seen above seas and large land masses.

"That's our twin planet, Zanarah," whispered Yildun. She also showed them the barren moon, which she explained orbited both planets in a figure eight pattern. Shen then urged them to leave before they were seen.

Yildun was leading the way down the ramp when a large dark creature swooped over them and grabbed Randir with a clawed talon.

Randir cried out in fear and surprise as the creature flew upwards into the night, beating wings creating gusts of air and ascending so quickly that the halfling's stomach tied up in knots. He was terrified that at any moment the dragon's claws would open and he would fall to his death.

Poor Randir-La squealed as she was dragged behind them. Her tiny body was spinning over and over in the swirling air, wings unable to gain purchase, but the halfling-fairy bond brought her high into the clouds.

Randir caught a glimpse of shiny jewelled-scales under the dragon's enormous wings and hopefully called out, "Asher?"

The dragon's piercing yellow eyes bore into his and he spoke harshly, "Foolish young halfling! Fendi and I spent hours negotiating with the centaurs and you risk it all by entering their sacred shrine! I should leave you behind with the centaur-younglings."

The dragon was clearly irritated and belched fire from its nostrils. Randir held tightly to the talon, scared that at any moment Ash would drop him to his death.

Randir-La finally got her wings flapping, catching up to her halfling who held her gently. "I told you this would lead to no good," said bossy Randir-La smugly. "You wouldn't listen." She flew right up in Randir's face and he angrily tried to swat her away.

"I forget how young you really are, halfling," Ash Dragon continued. "You look fully grown, however inside you are still a 17-year old boy out on an adventure. Very well; this once I will overlook your foolishness. Be warned that there will be no second chances. Do you understand me?" He loosened his grip on Randir.

"Y-y-yes Asher sir, I mean Ash Dragon sir," stammered the frightened halfling.

The dragon growled and gripped him more firmly. "I hope for all our sakes that your friends have made it back to their beds undetected. I expect double weapon's practice from you at dawn, before we travel. Now go and get some sleep. Goodness knows your head be in need of some common sense."

Ash Dragon had flown far from the pyramid during the lecture and now turned back towards the village. He seemed happy stretching his wings and once Randir had gotten over the shock of flying; he too found the experience enjoyable. Cradled in the dragon's sharp claws, Randir stretched out his arms to either side and felt a burst of exhilaration.

"I'm flying!" he cried gleefully, feeling an echo of exhilaration from Randir-La, and the big grey dragon gave a deep-throated chuckle.

After a while, the Village of the Sacred Shrine came into view and the dragon set Randir down near the orchard. The halfling tried to watch Asher shape-shift, but it was dark in the shadowy grove. Moments later, the tall mountain man walked towards him, yellow-green eyes glowing in the darkness.

Firmly gripping Randir's shoulder, Asher guided him back to the hut. The halfling crawled into his leafy bed beside Fendi and thought excitedly of his flight with Ash. The two dwarves snored nearby.

CHAPTER 5: TO DESOLATE CASTLE

The following morning, Asher had Randir practise with sword and longbow until his arms ached. Then the hunters packed their meagre belongings and gathered with the centaurs for the journey to the desert outpost. Sir Varnon insisted that they each carry three large water skins, for the journey would take many days.

They had difficulty extricating the dwarven brothers from the centaurs, for Raja enjoyed the village elders' stimulating conversations and he had an insatiable thirst for knowledge. Baja promised to return with him one day while Raja shook each centaur's hand for the third time, his bearded face glowing with happiness. When he finally joined his waiting companions he carried straw hats for their journey across the desert.

Baja had seemed a little dispirited after learning the centaurs cared little for ale or cards, so contented himself with impressing the centaur women with battle tales and demonstrations with the war hammer and dragon's tooth dagger. Evidently impressed, a group of pretty centaur women gathered to farewell the gregarious dwarf. They gave him three small sacks of caco beans and seeds to trade with other races.

Six centaurs had been chosen to carry the hunters across the desert. Asher, Sir Varnon, Daeron and Baja each had their own mount, whilst Raja and the halflings shared.

Sienna rode behind Fendi, securing their bedrolls to her back, along with her bow and arrows. Piebald Saiph lowered his front legs to allow the small halflings to mount, but with no saddle, Fendi held tightly to his chest while Sienna slipped her arms around Fendi's waist, much to his halflings' delight. Fendi experienced a flush of pleasure at the pretty huntress holding him.

Two extra centaurs were chosen to escort them, carrying extra water supplies and two large tents to protect them from sand storms. To the halflings' surprise Yildun was one of them, looking proud to be helping the travellers, who greeted her warmly.

The red-haired Fornax was in charge of the journey. King Apheratz who was preparing his warriors for the coming battle, bade them a solemn goodbye as they left, heading toward the Great Eastern Desert.

The first day's travel passed quickly. Leaving the dry forest, they galloped through grasslands and insect mounds which gradually became a sandy red desert, stretching as far as the eye could see.

Fornax seemed tireless and set a fast pace. He carried the heavy mountain man on his back, daring anyone to complain about the exertion, and Randir thought the other centaurs were probably a little scared of their quick-tempered leader.

Fendi and Sienna were enjoying their close company on Saiph's back. It was difficult to ride without a saddle and Sienna had to grip Fendi's waist tightly to keep from falling off. Fendi finally overcame his fear of talking to her and they spent hours discussing their journey and their lives back in the South Lands. Sienna worried about what she would do upon their return, for she flatly refused to live with her possessive uncle in Greendale. Fendi said that she was welcome to stay with him or Randir. Fendi's mother would be all alone, now that Old Fandri was gone and the huntress would be a welcome addition to the family.

Sienna was a little scared about being an addition to Fendi's family. Perhaps life with Randir's large family might be a lot less complicated, she thought. Still, she was developing strong feelings for Fendi, so would cross that bridge when she came to it. Meanwhile she enjoyed having an excuse to hug him tightly as Saiph trotted through the red sand dunes.

When they finally halted at sunset, the travellers were drenched in sweat from the long day's ride. Fornax didn't allow a moment's rest before making camp and the weary travellers struggled to raise the two large tents. He ordered the centaurs to share one of the tents before warning the hunters they would be resuming their journey in just four hours' time.

"Well, I guess we have been excused," said Sir Varnon, a wry smile on his ruddy face. Entering the tent he shrugged his backpack to the ground. "It is fortunate the huntress and I caught a dozen hoppers this morning while Randir and Asher did weapons practice. The centaurs may not like it, but we have to eat and I do not think we would survive on the insects they use for food. I would wager they are digging right now for scorpions in the sand," he said caustically.

The knight settled to the floor and opened his backpack to reveal their catch. "Ash, if you would be so kind?" he said, handing the large brace to the mountain man.

Asher returned shortly with roasted hoppers and Randir greeted him with a smile, gratefully sharing them out.

"Just remember they have to last us a few days, for there be little food in this sand bowl," Ash said. Randir's smile faded rapidly and he ate only a small amount before placing the wrapped remainder carefully in his backpack. However they were not without food for the hunters had brought a reasonable amount of fruit and corn bread with them. They were careful to ration their water, for Saiph told them it would be three days before they could refill their water skins.

After the meal, the fairies sang songs of recuperation to the weary halflings, and Raja joined in with his healing pan pipes. The desert cooled quickly after sundown and Fendi remembered it was winter in this part of the world.

"We didn't bring any blankets on our journey, only our thin bedrolls," he said with dismay as he moved towards the tent corner where the three fairies had curled up on their newly-formed toadstools.

With a coy smile, Sienna said, "Then I guess we'll have to share our body warmth so we don't freeze."

Fendi was half excited and half scared at the suggestion and lay down between Randir and Sienna on thin blankets. Sienna turned away from Fendi but wiggled backwards until she touched his chest. Fendi

93

uncertainly held his breath, but when Sienna reached back and pulled his arm across her, his heart beat like a drum and he buried his face into her long, dark hair.

The fairies' light glowed faintly in the still desert night and the hunters slept deeply after their long day. It did indeed get cold, but they didn't notice for the hunters' tent was warm enough when they huddled together.

At midnight, Fornax rudely woke them, "Come on you hunters. We need to cover a lot of ground before the sun rises."

They rode through the night and the next morning. During the hottest part of the day they rested in the tents, but still felt the sun's blistering heat beating down on their shelter. The following two days and nights passed in similar fashion until the parched travellers eventually reached the oasis at twilight on the third day. As darkness fell they could just make out a large lake surrounded by palm trees.

Large flocks of squawking screechers greeted them, which Raja explained was due to their annual migration from the cooler regions in the north. "They'll be heading south to the Zanzi Grasslands. They feast on the desert fruit here so I hope they have left some for us."

Up ahead, Fornax was conferring with a group of men camped around a fire near the lake. He bade the hunters come forward, introducing them to a dark man named Daku who wore little clothing.

Daku spoke to them in a friendly though strangely accented, voice, "Welcome to Humbybore. You may dine with us and fill your water skins. Your leader tells me that you have far to travel and will only stay a short while. Please rest and enjoy our water."

Asher spoke for the hunters, "Thank-you Daku, we appreciate your hospitality. Are these birds alright to eat? We'd be happy to catch some for you."

Daku replied, "Yes, unfortunately they breed prolifically and are eating our fruit. By all means catch some if you can."

Randir and Sienna obliged with their longbows and soon had enough for a meal. A few centaurs like Yildun and Saiph shared them with the hunters, but most dined only on insects.

Fornax allowed them only a two-hour rest by the calm waters, for he was anxious to continue their nightly trek.

*   *   *

No sooner had Daeron laid his head on a mound of desert grass, when a vision overcame him. *He saw his elven Princess, Shari-Rose deep in thought, looking into her mirror. He knew she was imprisoned in the harsh land of Vergash and his heart was moved to see her. Her hair hung unkempt and she looked frustrated, but there was still a spark of fire in her clear green eyes, and Daeron realised she was listening to a conversation in another room.*

She touched the beautiful elven jewel attached to the base of her neck. To Daeron's surprise and joy, the crystal rose-shaped gem had been fully restored, glowing with a multitude of colours that streamed from the elf's slender fingertips; light patterns that added colour to her plain white dress.

Concentrating, Daeron heard voices seemingly coming from within the crystal and wondered if this was the first time Shari-Rose had used the jewel to eavesdrop, or if it was a habit of hers from Reloria. He heard two deep voices, which he recognised as the giant Emperor Chi'garu and his General Ga'hiji.

The Cyclops Emperor was saying, "I'll give those useless Vergai one more week to conquer the desert and then win or lose, they can start on the western shield. Send word to our battleships to prepare to sail for the western shores of Reloria. Failure in the desert must not delay my plans to conquer these lands."

General Ga'hiji's voice argued, "But my Emperor, how will we know if they have succeeded if you stop the daily portals? Also our ships won't be able to get through with the shield still holding."

"Ga'hiji, you displease me. I have ordered and I will be obeyed! You will go through the western portal yourself and ensure the shield is destroyed. Capture the wizard or elf guardian who holds it and bring him to me. I will have this magic for myself," thundered the Cyclop's booming voice. "Do not fail me or you will meet the same fate as your predecessor."

Ga'hiji grew silent and Daeron could only guess the horrible fate of the giant Emperor's last general. Through Shari-Rose's eyes, he had seen the giant leader burn her crystal rose with a white-hot beam of light from his large eye. This giant who sought to be a God was certainly someone to be feared.

Daeron had one last look at the beautiful Princess, before the vision ended and he blinked in the dark desert. His companions huddled round the fire while he told Asher the news. The mountain man was thoughtful at the giant's change in tactic.

"Well, I guess we can do little else for the moment, but continue to the desert outpost and pray that the Vergai have not managed to destroy the shield guardian there. Then we shall hasten to the elves and the west, which will leave precious little time in Flame Mountain to marshal our defences."

* * *

True to his word, Fornax pushed the centaurs hard across the sand until mid-morning and this continued for four more scorching days.

They finally approached Desolate Castle at dawn on the seventh day since leaving the Village of the Sacred Shrine and none too soon, for the centaurs were exhausted.

Except for the colour, Desolate Castle looked similar in design to the Lakehaven Castle, but it was built of red sandstone.

The centaurs watched with amazement as Asher transformed into the mighty Ash Dragon. The mountain man shimmered and grew hazy, to be replaced by a large grey dragon with emerald scales on his torso. His horned head stood many times as tall as the centaurs and smoke billowed from his nostrils.

Scouting out the castle, Ash Dragon reported back to Fornax and the hunters. "Aye, Vergai are swarming all over the place," his voice rasped. His yellow eyes glowed with passion and he continued, "There be but one main entrance, wide open and unguarded. I suggest a frontal assault while I swoop in overhead with the dwarves."

Baja and Raja looked perturbed at this idea. Baja exclaimed in disgust, "You mean to throw me on the enemy like a sack of potatoes? I would not survive the humiliation!"

Raja nodded in agreement.

Ash Dragon turned those steely yellow eyes on the dwarves and his voice was low and gravely, "If you choose not to follow my orders, you will be left here in the desert to rot."

Baja turned pale and quickly replied, "Well of course, wise dragon, it's a very good battle plan. We could have them all down before the centaurs and others even get inside. What are we waiting for?" He brandished Shakti, his war hammer, while his brother darted next to him wielding a two-headed battle axe. The dwarves hurriedly mounted the dragon, and their long red hair streamed out behind them as he took flight.

The dragon swooped low over the desert sands with the dwarves yelping in alarm as he skimmed the castle wall. They jumped to the ground and the dragon created a fireball, ready to attack.

Sir Varnon led the others charging through the open gates, centaurs following with tridents in hand. There were loud noises of the skirmish within and the hunters ran full pelt into the courtyard, before stopping in surprise.

Dozens of Vergai were lying strewn on the ground and a pungent odour assaulted the senses. Many seemed to have died of natural causes and the charred remainder had been quickly dispatched by the dwarves and dragon.

Sir Varnon actually looked a little disappointed. The flush of anticipation was on his cheeks, "Could you not have saved some for me?"

A wooden door to the keep creaked open and the knight rushed over with sword drawn. Thirty Vergai rushed toward him with spiked maces and the dwarves gave a loud battle cry before joining the knight in the fray.

Baja thumped his war hammer into the ground, shouting, "Shakti, thump!"

All the Vergai were felled by an invisible magical wave, giving the hunters precious seconds to form a fighting line before the enemy sprang to their feet, morning stars outstretched.

Fendi's heart was beating fast as he rushed in with his sword drawn and attacked a scaly creature twice his height, ducking as a morning star whizzed through the air where his head had been. He bravely swung his sword but it bounced off the creature's tough chest. The Vergai hissed and swung at the halfling, striking a glancing blow which tore open Fendi's shoulder. He managed a weak thrust at the Vergai warrior's stomach, then Daeron was by his side, longsword deftly slicing the enemy's throat. Green blood poured forth and the creature fell sideways to the ground.

Fendi heard Sienna scream as he collapsed behind the agile elf, blood squirting from his open shoulder wound. He could feel his fairy somewhere close by, pouring all her healing energy into sealing off the severed artery. Fendi-La landed on his shoulder aglow with magical powers. They were both weakened by the pain and blood loss, but he was aware of the bleeding subsiding as the brave fairy knitted the artery together to save both their lives.

Meanwhile, fighting continued all around, and as the Vergai surged forward into the castle courtyard, Fendi's vision narrowed to dozens of scaly green feet and legs.

Then two small pairs of hands grabbed the wounded halfling, who looked up to see Randir and Sienna coming to his rescue. The knight, dwarves and elf all formed a protective fighting circle about him, while his friends dragged him out of the thickest fighting. Fendi gritted his teeth when Randir pulled his injured shoulder.

The halflings rested him against a shady wall near the dragon and resumed firing arrows into the enemy. The huntress' aim was remarkable, stopping scaly creatures in their tracks with well-placed shots through the throat. Randir's skill was developing and he wounded several creatures as well.

The dragon fought nearby with tooth and claw and controlled bursts of flame. He bit the head off one scaly opponent, spitting out vile green blood in disgust, before roasting the next creature foolish enough to attack him. One Vergai was impaled upon his spiked horns and tossed far into the desert.

Sir Varnon exchanged blows with a particularly ugly Vergai warrior, feinted to the left and then speared him under the arm with his broadsword. Next to him Baja disposed of another Vergai with a war hammer blow to the shoulder before slicing its throat with his dragon's tooth dagger. A short distance away Raja growled aggressively, trading blows with a fierce opponent, wielding his double-headed axe like he was born with it. Soon the Vergai's scarred head was rolling in the sand.

Daeron nimbly barred the doorway to stop the last two retreating Vergai. Instead they ran straight towards the dragon whose outstretched wings touched either side of the large courtyard. The enemy stopped dead in their tracks and Daeron's long blade put paid to one in the blink of an eye. The red-haired Fornax stepped forward, his forked trident skewering the final adversary. The centaur appeared surprised at the quick elimination of their fierce-looking foe, and glanced round, looking for more targets.

"Not bad," conceded the usually ill-tempered Fornax approvingly and the other centaurs bowed their heads in respect. A small pile of Vergai bodies also lay at their hooves beneath the bronze tridents.

"I should think that strong praise coming from you, centaur," commented Sir Varnon, as he cleaned his sword and sheathed it. He ran a hand through sweaty blond curls.

Meanwhile, Raja approached the injured Fendi and Fendi-La, quickly appraising the injury to his shoulder. The dwarf stowed his axe, brought out a small set of pan pipes, and healing music started to knit together the chipped bone and open wound. Then Sienna washed Fendi's arm and tied a bandage around to protect the newly-healed skin.

Ash divided the companions into two teams to search the rest of the castle.

"There's no need to search further," said a small voice nearby. The dragon looked down to see a short young woman, with black hair fashioned into scruffy buns either side of her head, with eyes an amazing violet colour. She wore a simple dress of black cotton, with bare feet and no discernible weapon. In her hand she carried a thin white stick about as long as her forearm. "The remaining invaders are either dead or dying from lack of water. Thank-you for finishing this lot off for me, although of course I'd have done it myself if you weren't here. Your assistance was appreciated, so come on in out of the hot sun."

Turning abruptly on her heel, she disappeared through the doorway into the keep.

"Well, that was odd," said Asher. The mountain man was bending over a Vergai with a knife in hand. "She's right about one thing. These invaders won't be troubling us again. I'm just surprised she survived against them. I'm guessing from the white wand that she is probably our wizard and well able to defend herself."

He tucked the knife in his belt and strode towards the keep. "Fornax, would you be so kind as to hold the courtyard while we're gone?" The centaur gave a nod, looking slightly less grumpy than previously. The other centaurs ranged round him, tridents at the ready, while the hunters followed Asher into the cool of the castle.

The little lady led them down a flight of stairs that ended at a blank wall, then waving the white wand, she murmured something under her breath and the solid stone abruptly transformed into a sturdy oaken door. "Welcome to the real Desolate Castle. I am Violetta, apprentice to Wizard Nnald. Please call me Vi. My master is almost blind and deaf from extreme old age, so make sure you speak loudly and clearly, and be aware he may forget the start of the sentence by the time he reaches the end of it."

Vi opened the door and led the hunters down a long flight of stairs which flattened out into an even longer tunnel through solid bedrock. Her voice droned on and on as they passed wall-mounted glowing blue torches and tunnels branching in all directions.

"These caves under the castle were built over many decades by the gnomes who live here and extend for miles below the desert floor. One even goes west to where centaurs deliver food through a trap door. Don't ask me why, but gnomes like to live underground. They take up a lot of space with their scientific laboratories and are always conducting weird and wonderful experiments. Did you like the castle overhead?

Desolate Castle is such a good name for it. It being all by itself you know and in quite a desolate location. I always thought that was a really clever name and....."

The hunters tuned out to the young apprentice's incessant babble and looked instead at the gnomes they were passing. Standing around the size of a halfling with unusually pink skin and ears jutting out like saucers from the sides of their pointed hats, they had but three stubby fingers and a thumb on each hand and fabric boots on their feet. Their long tunic shirts and tight hose were of many colours and patterns and appeared to have been donned with no thought to their other garments.

One of the gnomes wearing a yellow hat, blue and green striped shirt and purple tights beckoned them over. Vi gave a sigh and paused her endless dialogue to join him. She started to introduce the hunters, but stopped when she realised she didn't know any of their names. Asher calmly interjected, "I'd love to see what you're boiling there friend gnome, but we are here on a matter of some urgency. We need to speak with the wizard, but hopefully, we can see you afterwards."

Vi looked a little disappointed, but led them through the cave full of bubbling pots and tubes running haphazardly around the room. The next cave contained more gnomes working on mechanisms of cogs and wheels; then another filled with a floating canvas bag over a fire; and yet a further one where various substances were being mixed together in glass beakers. There was a loud pop as they passed this last room and a gnome looked up at them through a haze of smelly green smoke. Fendi noticed Baja and Raja sneaking into one of the gnomes' laboratories and briefly wondered what they were up to.

At the end of this passage was the wizard's house. He was snoring away in a rocking chair, his white beard so long it touched the floor. By the look of his wrinkles, he was the oldest wizard that any of them had ever seen, indeed apart from Sir Varnon and Daeron, the **only** wizard that any of them had seen. He certainly looked the part, wearing a midnight-blue cloak and hat covered in silvery stars and a black wand topped with a shining white orb rested idly across his lap.

Fendi whispered quietly to Sienna, "I can't see this old wizard being able to create a portal to rescue Shari-Rose. He looks too defenceless to be of any help to us. The best we can hope for is to stop the Vergai coming here to capture him." The huntress nodded in agreement.

The apprentice was babbling on again about the wizard being nearly a thousand years old and how the elven shield had been his suggestion in the first place. Yet she seemed very fond of him and straightened the rug over his knees as he slept. He yawned, trying to roll over in the rocking chair and his pointed hat fell off to reveal a shiny bald head. With a snort, he opened his eyes.

"What, where...oh, it's you," he said, gazing intently at Vi with clouded eyes. "I was having the nicest dream about my childhood in Nnanell and..." he broke off speaking abruptly, realising there was a crowd of people in his living room. "Ah, we have visitors. I am Wizard Fitzwinkle Nnald, keeper of the Eastern shield outpost. I do prefer to be known as Wizard Nnald, as Fitzwinkle is not a distinguished name for someone of my advanced years."

The halflings gave a small tittery chuckle at the mention of his first name, though the wizard appeared not to hear them. Asher stepped forward to make the introductions. "I am Asher Grey from Flame Mountain," he said politely.

"Masher Hay, what a strange name," said the nearly deaf wizard.

"This is Sir Varnon of the Diagro Plains."

"Pleased to meet you Sir Marlon."

"And Daeron, of the elven forest."

"Glare on?   Now that's a really unusual name," continued the Wizard Nnald as he shook each hand in turn.   The halflings could barely contain their mirth as the wizard incorrectly repeated each name.   Randir was holding an aching stitch in his side while Fendi and Sienna tried to hide tears of laughter.

Asher gave a warning look with yellow-green eyes and continued, "Here be Baja and Raja of Diamond City. Actually, they're not here! Where are our dwarves?"

"I think they've gone to play with the gnomes," replied Fendi quietly.

The old mage looked as though he was about to fall asleep again.   Asher hurriedly added, "And Fendi, Sienna and Randir of the south."

The wizard looked perplexed and said, "Bendy antenna reindeer mouth?"

This was more than the halflings could bear, and laughter burst forth, to be echoed round the room.

Young Violetta joined in the merriment and when the laughter had abated, she said, "The gnomes are working on a listening device to help with his hearing. The most recent remedy they tried caused his hair to fall out. Luckily his beard stayed intact, so he doesn't seem to notice that he is bald yet. I'm hoping the wizard will allow me to take the wizard's exam soon and then I can run the outpost for him. As it is, I have to wake him every day to perform the spell and then he falls back to sleep. I know I'm ready to be a wizard and I'm strong in all the elements, which is quite a rare thing," she added smugly.

Sir Varnon tried to speak, but the apprentice continued to prattle on, "Come and I will feed you all and then we can devise a plan to prevent the Vergai from coming into the castle. There will be another group of about ten to twenty coming through the portal at the third turn after noon. I was thinking about a fire-ball spell to throw into the portal. That ought to slow them down."

The old wizard appeared to have fallen asleep again, so the hunters followed Vi back through the tunnels.

"This is very frustrating!" said Asher to Sir Varnon and Raja, who had just re-joined the group. "I was sure this would have been the wizard we needed to fulfil the prophecy and help us on our quest."

Raja answered him, "Remember we require a mage with three or more powers." He turned to Violetta, "Does Wizard Nnald have three powers?"

"No, he is only an air wizard," Vi replied. "There are only three mages and they make up the council back home in Nnanell, the greatest of whom is Grand Mage Nnarndam, our leader. He hasn't been to Reloria in my lifetime. Anyway, I'm very good at magic and can help you, I'm sure. Why only the other day I..."

Asher stopped listening and spoke to Randir, "We must continue our search elsewhere. The Elven Jewel and the fate of all Reloria depend on us fulfilling this quest. Let us go to Conlaoch Diarmada and seek the Elven Queen's counsel. We must find a way to contact this Grand Mage and seek his aid."

Undeterred by being shunned, Vi grabbed Randir by the arm, insisting on hearing about his travels as they passed by strange gnomish inventions and continued down a long corridor towards her living quarters. They found the elusive dwarves along the way and a gnome handed Raja a large pot of hot caco drink. Baja had apparently traded a bag of caco seeds for some explosive balls in a sack.

"Be careful with those explosives, or you'll blow yourself up instead of the Vergai," called an elderly gnome wearing garish clothes covered in singed holes.

"I'll nurse them like a baby," promised Baja with a grin, running after his friends.

Randir gave Violetta a brief account of their adventures over a delicious lunch of meat pie and honeyed roots. By the time two gnomish ladies brought dessert, he had reached the story of Te Mātau and was describing the little furmal who had befriended him.

"I really miss Kulana," he said sadly. "She was such a nice little companion." He helped himself to a generous portion of stewed fruits and custard while Vi questioned him further. The apprentice seemed quite absorbed in his tale and made appreciative murmurs as she sipped her mug of hot caco.

Asher then asked the question that had been puzzling most of the hunters, "Violetta, how do you have such delicious food in the middle of a desert?"

The little apprentice gave a cheeky smile and her beautiful violet eyes twinkled. "Well, don't tell the gnomes that you heard it from me, but they invented an ice machine to keep food cool in the desert. Well actually, I invented the cooling spell, it's a type of air shield that I wrap round the box to keep heat out. The gnomes make ice in their laboratories. I'm thinking about selling my invention to the elves and humans, if I ever get out of the desert. I am so bored here, with nothing to do and only a blind and deaf wizard to talk to.

 "I do like the gnomes, but they use such complicated words that I can barely understand them. It's all chemical elements, mathematics, and things that go 'boom' by accident. I am a little frightened by them sometimes, but there is one invention I would like to try. It's a flying machine so I could leave here one day when I finally pass the wizard trials and ..."

Asher raised his hand, interrupting the incessant dialogue. "My dear Violetta, we are grateful for your hospitality, but could we please speak with the gnomish inventor of the flying machine?"

The apprentice bobbed her head, saying, "Of course Asher Grey. I shall go and get Heikki. He will be thrilled to tell you all about...." Her voice trailed off down into the tunnel and the hunters shared a sigh of relief.

"I am so glad we are seeking a wizard and not an apprentice," declared Fendi fervently. "She just does not stop talking!"

Daeron had a thoughtful look on his pale face and said, "Did you hear the wizard's name? Nnald, from the land of Nnanell. I think that must be where all the wizards originally came from. He may be related to the wizards who are being used to create the portal. If so, this will be tricky. Now we know that if we destroy the portal, then we may be killing his kin. If the Vergai can do no harm here, then perhaps we should leave them be."

The hunters mulled over this until their talkative host came back with an oddly-dressed gnome named Heikki. He wore a red hat, which went nicely with his red shoes, but clashed awfully with an orange and purple swirled tunic, blue belt and green leggings. Fendi smiled at the thought that perhaps gnomes were colour-blind.

A trio of gnomes followed them, excited to be meeting strangers, especially the tiny female, Tarja. Any hope of gnomish women's fashion sense disintegrated at the sight of her long white hair arranged in two plaits with orange ribbon, a red and blue striped dress, orange and green tights and purple belt. The colours were giving Fendi a headache.

When Violetta asked Heikki to explain his flying machine to the hunters, the colourful gnome stepped forward, tucking his white beard into his belt and unrolled a large parchment onto the table. The diagram showed a balloon suspended above a fire and a steering mechanism attached to wings pulled by levers. Underneath the contraption was a large basket for carrying passengers. The hunters looked on in horror and disbelief.

"There is no way that thing could fly!" declared Randir. "It looks like a death-trap. Even if it got off the ground, how would you keep it in the air?"

"It does work," declared Violetta indignantly. "Heikki did a trial just this past week and he flew around the castle. I saw him do it." The gnome nodded proudly at his achievement.

"We **are** in a hurry, and the gnomes are renowned inventors," said Asher thoughtfully, absentmindedly stroking his short goatee. "Let's see the invention in action before we judge it." The hunters exchanged disbelieving looks, but deferred to their leader, while Heikki beaming with pleasure, led them up the long tunnel to the surface.

They trooped into the courtyard, where the centaurs looked up expectantly.

"What's happening?" asked Fornax impatiently, looking hot and bothered in the desert heat. The centaurs were still tired from climbing sand dunes all night, and were lying in the shade, tridents within easy reach.

Asher answered him mildly, "We are here to see if this goblin's flying machine can take us to the elves. It could save a long trip westwards across the desert if it does! Well then, Heikki, where is this flying machine?"

The gnomes went over to what appeared to be solid stone, pressed a hidden lever and a false floor popped up revealing a large cavity underneath. Assisted by the hunters, four gnomes pulled a sizable gondola from the hole, large enough to comfortably hold ten people. Next was a strange device, which Heikki called the propeller, accompanied by cables and a series of wheels and chains which the gnome called a cycle.

Last of all came the balloon itself; a massive ovoid made of double sewn material, the stitching coated in wax to prevent leaks. The gnomes assembled the entire contraption in the castle courtyard, tying it together with thick cables.

As they were inflating the balloon with hot air from the furnace, a large black portal appeared, surrounded by a flickering magical halo.

The centaurs bravely leapt into action with their bronze tridents, but were stopped short by a commanding call from the tiny wizard's apprentice. "Don't move!" she cried. To the companion's surprise she held a large ball of flickering lightning in her hands. She uttered an enchantment and hurled the lightning into the dark void. Screams sounded before the portal winked out of existence.

The centaurs raced forward with their tridents to battle the eight Vergai who had emerged from the portal. Snarling as they sensed defeat, the Vergai fiercely charged the horse-men, who hesitated momentarily. Asher drew his knives and led the hunters to join them. Sword and trident clashed against spiked morning stars and the Vergai were quickly forced into a corner.

"Yield and your lives shall be spared," called Sir Varnon honourably.

"Never!" replied eight raspy Vergai, swinging their maces wildly as they again rushed the hunters and centaurs. The battle was over quickly, for the outnumbered enemy ran into a seemingly solid wall of weapons and were speedily dispatched.

As the centaurs dragged the enemies' bodies away, those remaining in the courtyard slowly turned towards Violetta.

It was Fendi who broke the silence. "That was amazing magic, Vi! You really are going to be a wizard."

"I told you I was," she replied a little haughtily. "Who do you think does all the magic here anyway? The only thing Wizard Nnald does is the daily elven shield spell which I could do myself if I wanted too. He doesn't even realise that I run this place singlehandedly and I am very talented. I'm the most powerful apprentice I know by a long shot, so you really would benefit from my amazing skills. Boy, if you knew some of the things I can do, it would make your hair stand on end. So, can I go with you please?"

"No," said all eight hunters in unison. The tiny apprentice burst into tears and ran off into the castle. Fendi looked as though to follow her, but Sienna laid a gentle hand on his arm.

"Fendi, there's nothing you can say to make her feel any better," the huntress said kindly. "None of us could have endured her incessant talking for a day, let alone a whole voyage. The Ancient Oracle said that we have to find a mage to take us to Vergash, not a wizard's apprentice. I'm sure that we will find another. Obviously Wizard Nnald isn't up to the task. Our best bet is to seek help from the elves, who surely know some wizards who can help us."

The sombre mood was broken when Randir gave a cry of surprise. The hunters looked to see him pulling a grey furmal gently out of his backpack. "Kulana!" he said with delight. "However did you cross the desert? Were you inside my backpack the entire time? Surely not!"

The little furmal curled up around Randir's leg before running quickly up his outstretched arms and perching on his shoulder, making a tittering sound in his ear and rubbing her soft cheeks against his. "Yes, I have missed you too, sweet furmal. You must have been eating my food for you seem a little fatter than before."

Everyone laughed good-naturedly when Fendi added, "I can't believe you carried her here all this way without noticing her. No wonder your backpack always looks full. It started out full of food and now it's just full of furmal! We'll have to take her with us. We can't just leave her here in the desert. She must have doubled back to you when Rere returned to Te Mātau." The hunters gave cute Kulana a welcoming pat. One of the gnomes produced a yellow juju and she wasted no time gnawing on the juicy fruit.

CHAPTER 6: ADVENTURES ALOFT

"We're ready," Heikki called and the hunters turned as one to see the amazing flying machine. The fully inflated balloon floated high in the air, suspending a small machine and seat for the driver near the furnace. The balloon was colourful in typical gnomish style with clashing swirls and stripes of practically every colour. More than a man's height below, the large wicker basket also rose from the ground, restrained only by the centaurs holding the thick cables and tying them to sturdy iron fastenings in the castle walls. A steady stream of gnomes brought food and water for the departing hunters and centaurs.

"You better get in. We're ready to launch," cried the colourful Heikki as he pulled something over his red hat which covered his eyes, making them look twice as big.

"Goggles," he said, as if that explained the strange orange glass, embedded in a black mask. Everyone still seemed puzzled, so he explained, "It's to keep the sand out of my eyes while I steer the balloon."

"Alright, I'm sure these goggles are less of a concern than is this flying machine," Asher said. "Come on, brave hunters, time's a-wasting. We need to warn the elves and reach the western outpost before the invaders. In you go." He gave Sienna a hand up into the basket and the others reluctantly followed.

Asher turned to the red-hair centaur, "Thank-you for all your assistance Fornax. We'll see you on the Diagro Plains when you have made the great journey. Please give my greetings and thanks to King Alpheratz," he said holding out his hand.

Fornax gave a small bow and clasped hands with the mountain man. "It has been an interesting experience to be sure. Have faith in this gnome and his flying machine, for it is written in the stars that we'll meet again on the field of battle. Goodbye hunters. Do try and stay out of trouble."

The hunters watched as the centaurs galloped off into the evening desert, their hair and tails streaming behind them. Yildun and Saiph waved farewell before cresting the sand dunes and disappearing from sight.

The gnomes packed bags of food and drink into the basket to sustain them during their journey. The blonde-haired female, Tarja, said she'd looked for Violetta, but she must be sulking in one of the caves.

"Please give her our thanks," said Fendi. "She's a friendly host and we're sorry that we couldn't say goodbye." Asher gave him an approving clap on the shoulder, and when the gnomes untied the mooring cables, the balloon rose rapidly into the air.

The halflings looked down worriedly as Desolate Castle grew smaller and smaller in the vast desert below. Fendi cried out in alarm at their rapidly increasing altitude, but Randir's furmal jumped lightly across to the nervous halfling, giving him a reassuring hug with her furry tail while chattering in his ear. Strong winds were now swirling around them and the companions watched in horror as a wall of sand swept towards them from the east.

"Cover your eyes!" yelled Heikki from high above them. "It's a sandstorm."

The companions hid their faces as the biting sand overtook them, and the tiny fairies ducked into the halflings' pockets to avoid being blown away. Heikki let the balloon soar even higher above the desert where the wind sent it flying rapidly westward. "Thank goodness it's blowing in the right direction," he called down.

The strong wind continued on into the evening. The balloon now floated effortlessly above the sandstorm and the hunters watched the desert passing quickly below. Daeron's keen elven eyes spied desert sprites, pointing them out to his companions, for the wispy sand creatures were being blown about like tumbleweeds.

"There's something unnatural about this sandstorm," declared the elf. "I have lived my life around magic users and this feels like magic to me. Just look at the way those sprites are being tossed about. Usually they are the ones causing sandstorms, not the victims. Something's wrong here."

*   *   *

The winds continued through the night carrying the balloon swiftly westward. The night was moonless with only stars twinkling overhead. There was little room in the basket for the hunters to lie down, so they drifted off to sleep sitting upright, leaning against each other.

Fendi was woken at dawn by Randir tapping gently on his shoulder. He found Sienna curled on the floor of the basket with her head resting in his lap. Exchanging a smile with Randir he gently stroked her long brown hair, while little Fendi-La emerged from his shirt pocket, tugging her green hat straight on her tiny head. For once her toadstool bed had not grown.

"Good morning Fendi," the sweet fairy whispered. "What a wild night! Has the sandstorm eased up? It still feels as though we are moving quickly." She stretched to test her iridescent wings in the relatively still air of the basket. "I'm glad we're still in one piece. I thought that the wind last night might disintegrate us."

The companions were all stirring now and Sienna blinked slowly, looking up at Fendi from his lap. "Oh, I'm sorry Fendi," she said, a little embarrassed. "I must have slipped over in my sleep."

"It's alright Sienna," said Fendi shyly. "I'm happy to be of service." The two of them exchanged an affectionate smile and he hugged her as she sat up. "Now, where in Reloria are we?"

The dwarves peered over the edge of the basket. Baja turned, calling down to the halflings, "Well, you'll never believe this, but we're over halfway to the elves already. In a single night we've crossed the entire desert and some of the grasslands as well. It's incredible!"

The red-soiled grasslands were rolling below them when Asher's keen eyes spied a group of centaurs galloping over the plains. The grasslands continued expansively, until the Warrigal River could be seen, snaking out through the plains and disappearing into the forests on the horizon.

Raja said, "From my calculations, we will reach the elven city this afternoon if this strange wind continues."

"I concur," called Heikki's voice from above them. Everyone looked up to see the colourful gnome sitting in his seat above them next to the furnace. His long white hair and beard were streaming out in the wind. "It's a good thing too, as I only have enough coals up here to keep the furnace going today and then we will have to land to gather firewood. The balloon is a great way to travel, but it can't carry extra weight with you as well. I can't believe how far this wind has brought us in a single night." The gnome nimbly slid down a knotted rope to the passenger basket.

"Good morning to you all. I've brewed a nice pot of tea on the furnace and we've bread and cheese for a picnic breakfast."   He distributed cups and plates and after pouring tea from a truly colourful gnome teapot, he handed out containers of milk and honey. All of which made a delicious breakfast high above the Centaur Lands.

Sir Varnon was looking out across the grasslands, and, speaking as much to himself as anyone else, said, "It reminds me of home, the same boundless grasslands, although our soil is brown rather than red. It makes me homesick for my fair wife and children, for I have long been away and my father too will keenly await my return. I do wonder where this quest will take us next." For a brief moment the knight looked a little lost, shivering in the cool air, wearing only dark hose and the red tabard covered by his steel breastplate.

It had felt like summer in the desert, but now the companions were realising it was indeed winter in the northern lands.   The dwarves and Asher seemed oblivious to the elements. The mountain man wore his black leather through all the seasons and the dwarves their plain brown miner's clothes. Baja's wooden chest was tucked under his arm as usual, for he always guarded it, even in a hot air balloon high above the ground.

Daeron meanwhile was looking thoughtfully at Kulana snuggling close to Randir's cheek. The halfling had his hands wrapped tightly around a warm mug and his nose was half in the cup, as though trying to get that warm too. Sipping his drink, the elf said, "There's something different about Kulana this time, from when we left her at the centaur village. It's as if she were almost a different furmal. She looks very similar, but it's as though she has grown in size and not just from a good feed in your saddle bag. I can't quite put my finger it, but the difference is very subtle, like a slight change in hue. If anything, I would say that her personality is somewhat different than before. Just listen to her chattering away in your ear non-stop! She was more content before."

The little grey furmal tilted her head as though she were listening to Daeron. She stopped her chattering and nimbly jumped onto the picnic basket, glanced again at Daeron before curling herself into a ball.

Asher had taken an interest in the conversation, and then whispered, "Strange indeed," into the elf's ear, taking an interest in the conversation. "She reminds me very much of a talkative wizard's apprentice we left behind. We never saw them both at the same time, did we?"

Daeron nodded and deftly changed the subject, "Do you know who the shield keeper at the western outpost is?"

Asher shook his head and replied, "It be not far from Flame Mountain, but I've never been there. We mountain men are busy squabbling amongst ourselves or raiding the Diagro Plainsmen."

Sir Varnon gave a dry laugh, "You have that right. They do not seem to know much about the world around them and what we try to protect. Where were they when the Vergai invaded and the truces between elves and men were made? They were fighting over a woman or admiring their reflections. You are the first decent one I have met; a man who fights for more than just his own and goes to the aid of strangers; a man I would fight beside in any battle."

"Thank-you friend," said Asher and clapped the knight on the shoulder. "Do you know the western shield keeper's name?"

Laughing heartily, Sir Varnon replied, "I do indeed. He is the keeper of the great Shield of Reloria and father to Princess Shari-Rose, whom we are charged with rescuing. He is Crown-Prince Celdar-Moon, younger brother to the Elven Queen. He might be a little arrogant and difficult to speak with, but overall he is a just elf and is second only in magic to his daughter. When I accepted this quest from the Ancient Oracle to save Reloria, I understood the importance of the Prince and his daughter to our lands. Without them the Vergai would slaughter us all, for we are peaceful people and seek only to protect our own."

Daeron gave a small laugh, "Peaceful, you call it? You knights and mountain men have been sworn enemies for generations." He raised a hand in a gesture of peace at the looks of indignation radiating from the flushed faces of both Asher and the knight. "Be calm humans; there's no need to demonstrate your quick tempers here. I admire your unlikely truce and hope you can use your friendship to help us band the humans together against the Vergai. Goodness knows, we'll need every man we can muster to defeat the hordes of battleships heading our way."

There was silence for a moment, as they considered the impending Vergai invasion of the west lands. Raja was the first to speak and naturally his question was a thoughtful one, "Daeron, you call Prince Celdar-Moon the Crown-Prince, yet he is only the Queen's brother. Is she unable to have children of her own to succeed the throne?"

The elf nervously stroked his hair before he replied, "Well, my friends, it is an embarrassing elven secret, but you risk your lives for us here, so I believe you deserve to know. Queen Liara-Star has ruled for many years as you may know, and her late consort, King Phelaeron-Sky was quite ancient. They had three children many years ago, but to their great shame, none of the royal offspring had any magical abilities. This made them common elves and ineligible to succeed the throne. The duty now falls to Crown-Prince Celdar-Moon, who I have to admit should make a fine ruler one day."

"What happened to the other royal elves," asked Fendi-La, a slight flush of embarrassment on her cheeks as Fendi gave her a pat of encouragement.

Daeron smiled at the caring fairy and replied, "The prince and princesses live in the great forest and have become artisans of high renown. The Queen is very proud of them of course, but as they have no magical talent, their lifespans can't be expected to exceed two hundred years. Sadly, they must be approaching that now. The Queen's delight is her niece, Shari-Rose and she'll surely be devastated to learn of her kidnapping. I'm sure she will aid us in our quest."

*   *   *

It was late morning when they reached the Great Elven Forest, stretching far across the northern lands of Reloria, separating the east and west lands. To the south the northern arm of the Warrigal River disappeared into the forest, to the north were farmlands.

The elven forest was dense with a variety of extremely tall trees. Those on the outer fringes of the forest were bare of leaves for the winter, but further in, the trees were lush and verdant while the inner forest trees were fully laden with fruits, flowers and nuts, seemingly unaffected by the cold winter. The fairies in particular couldn't wait for the flying machine to land and see what magic kept them evergreen.

The balloon began to descend quite rapidly and Randir called to the gnome above them, "Heikki, we're about to hit the trees. Can you take us up a little higher?"

The gnome peered down at the halfling with a terrified look on his face. "I've run out of wood and the furnace is empty. I'm sorry, but we're about to crash land. Hang on to the basket, we're in for a bumpy ride." The hunters grabbed the handles on the basket, as the balloon started deflating and the basket roughly brushed the treetops. Fendi put a protective arm around Sienna, who buried her head in his chest, and closing their eyes, they braced themselves for the impact.

Randir tried to grab Kulana, but the spritely furmal scampered up the knotted rope to Heikki's pilot chair and sat on the petrified gnome's cap as he cringed, head between his knees. Twittering in furmal-speak she raised a paw and the balloon began rising again as a roaring fire sprung up in the empty furnace.

The relieved hunters gave a mighty cheer, but Daeron nimbly scaled the rope and picked the furmal up by her brown fluffy tail. "I think the game is up, Violetta. Reveal yourself."

He tossed her down to Asher, who caught her and quickly placed her on the basket floor. The halflings watched in amazement as the furmal quickly transformed herself back to her former self - the wizard's apprentice, now clad in a long black dress. She apprehensively darted looks at the sombre faces of Asher, Sir Varnon and Daeron.

It was Baja who broke the tension with a huge, dwarven belly-laugh, his long beard shaking with mirth, exclaiming, "Well, dragon's tooth, if you aren't the best good luck charm I've ever had, Violetta. That was brilliant!" He surprised Vi with a bear hug and patted her little black hair buns.

Raja, Heikki and the halflings all thanked the stow-a-away apprentice, though Daeron and the humans looked unsure whether to be happy or angry. Yet without her they might have all been killed.

Violetta smiled happily but avoided looking at the elf and humans. She launched into her usual babbling speech, "Thank-you. It is so wonderful to be sharing your adventures. Does this mean that I can come and be one of the Hunters of Reloria? I'd really like to. I am almost a wizard, you know. I just have to go to the wizard city and take the tests and then I will be one. I have abilities in each of the five magical elements: I can do spells with fire, air, water, land and shape." The chatty apprentice took a hurried breath and continued, "Did you like my shape-shifting? Now that's a rare spell you know, and then I did a combined fire and air spell to rescue the balloon. That's very difficult, you know. I can also do water spells to make an ice shield and make it rain and...."

Her voice petered out when Asher Grey's shadow loomed over her. Bending low until his nose almost touched hers, his strange yellow-green eyes stared until her violet eyes widened in fright. After a long silence, he said plainly, "Unless there is a spell to stop you talking, you'll be spending the rest of this journey as a furmal."

She nervously gulped and nodded her head several times. Somewhat chastened, she quietly sat on the floor of the big basket and the three fairies gathered around to comfort her. At least **they** were mightily impressed, and their retelling of her magical prowess soon returned her smile.

*   *   *

The hunters resumed watching the great forest below and at length saw the floating elven city of Conlaoch Diarmada. Built of gleaming white marble with a slight rosy hue, the city defied gravity, hanging among the fluffy clouds above a grassy clearing. Elegant arches linked a series of towers of differing heights with rose-bud spires. Raja explained that Conlaoch Diarmada had been made by wizards thousands of years ago. It was very beautiful and looked as if it were carved from a single, immense piece of marble. Majestic waterfalls fell from the base of the city to be lost in the clouds below.

Violetta and the fairies gathered on the edge of the wicker basket to ooh and ah at the amazing sight, particularly the masses of flowering trees ringing the clearing below.

"I can't wait to get down there and talk to the trees," whispered Fendi-La to her friends.

"I'd like to see the animals too," Sienna-Li said, flying off the edge of the basket and brushing the tops of the trees with his toes while the balloon gently floated along. Gleefully Fendi-La and Randir-La danced after him with their tiny bells tinkling, while Vi became a black-bird with violet wings, who joined the fairies' game, darting and swooping through the beautiful elven forest.

Heikki was working furiously aloft to steer their balloon to a safe landing. His bulbous feet were pedalling to make propellers turn, pulling the rudder cable with one hand and a lever releasing air from a vent with the other. The flying machine brushed the top of an impossibly-high waterfall, before passing through the clouds, bumping to the ground in a large clearing.

While landing, the hunters spied a young elf maiden patting a rare unicorn at the edge of the clearing. A circlet of flowers crowned her wavy brown hair and she wore a beautiful green silk dress. Her back was turned to them as she laid her head on the unicorn's white mane; she was stroking the creature's horn, when the thump of the balloon basket landing a short distance away startled them. The unicorn whinnied, and dashed off into the safety of the forest, while the surprised elf turned to see the balloon slowly deflating and Daeron saw her pretty face change expressions from to shock to wonder.

"Cassie-Belle!" he exclaimed in sudden recognition, leaping gracefully from the basket. She saw him too and ran nimbly across the grass towards him. They met in the middle of the field full of wildflowers, where Daeron picked her up by the waist and spun her around with glee.

"It's so good to see you. You are recovered from your injuries?" he asked at the same time as she said, "Oh, how I've missed you Daeron! Where have you been?" They both laughed and Cassie-Belle surprised them both by giving him a soft kiss on the lips. For the briefest of seconds, Daeron returned her kiss, before pulling away.

Adopting a grim expression, he said, "I beg your pardon, my Lady. I forgot my position for a second. It will not happen again." The longing in his eyes betrayed his emotions, when he gazed into Cassie-Belle's pale blue eyes, but then he looked to the ground as tears welled up in her pretty face. "It is marvellous to see you again, dear Lady," he added formally, "I am so pleased that you are fully recovered and returned home."

Cassie-Belle then looked past Daeron to the strange group of people watching from the balloon's basket. "Oh my," she said in surprise and a touch of embarrassment. Looking from one to the next, her gaze rested on the dwarves and Asher, "I've met you before, haven't I. You're Baja and Raja and I can't recall the name of your friend...."

"Asher Grey of Flame Mountain," the mountain man said with a bow. "The halflings are Fendi, Randir and Sienna who saved your lives at Lakehaven. This is Sir Varnon, son of King Varl and heir to the Diagro throne. Our gnomish friend here is Heikki, who has kindly brought us here in his flying contraption, and the black and violet bird there is Violetta, a shape-shifting wizard's apprentice. We bear urgent news for Queen Liara-Star. Would you be so good as to lead us to her?"

Cassie-Belle curtsied in greeting to the hunters and led the way toward the castle. Holding tightly to Daeron's arm, she whispered, "It is forbidden to bring non-elves to Conlaoch Diarmada, unless they are invited by the Queen, but I could request an audience on your behalf."

"If it were not so urgent, I would agree with you, my Lady," Daeron replied, "but unfortunately the western outpost is under attack, so we must insist on this meeting. I'm sure the Queen will want to meet with all of us and hear of our quest to rescue her niece, Shari-Rose."

As they approached the elegant city, the hunters marvelled at the floating structure far above the meadow, for not even a shadow betrayed the floating castle's existence. "Only true-hearted allies of the elves can actually see Conlaoch Diarmada," Cassie-Belle explained.

The companion's way was blocked by four green cloaked guards, bearing the silver leaf crest, who raced out from nearby trees. When the command: "Halt, in the name of the Queen," rang out, several elven bowmen who appeared from the trees, aimed arrows at the hunters. Meanwhile, the four elven guards drew long swords, clearly ready to use them.

Asher gave a nod to the knight.

Sir Varnon boldly stepped forward, speaking loudly and clearly: "Well met, friend elves. I am Sir Varnon, Prince of the Diagro Plains and I have urgent tidings for your Queen. Please allow me an audience with her."

The young elf guard relaxed his tense position and bowed in greeting, "Ah, yes your Highness. You are expected and your news keenly awaited. You may enter Conlaoch Diarmada."

To the hunters' relief he re-sheathed his sword and handed them each a delicate-looking flower. The second the hunters grasped the stem, they floated high into the air towards the Elven palace, landing gently on wide marble steps. The petals of the flower then turned into tiny pixies, who kissed the fairies and flew off into the forest below.

CHAPTER 7: CONLAOCH DIARMADA

The hunters were struck speechless by the incredible beauty of the magical palace. They followed the guard through a series of elegant marble corridors and curved staircases to the unusual open-air throne room built on a circular tower. The room was contained within a low, wavy wall, and in the centre, a shallow pool, whose glowing silvery water perfectly reflected the fluffy white clouds and the gently curving towers. The hunters edged forward toward the pool, gazing at the reflections while they waited, but Daeron's eyes were searching for Cassie-Belle who, to his disappointment, had left the room to wait on the Queen.

After a short while, Queen Liara-Star appeared. Clad in flowing clothes that enhanced her graceful stature, she was preceded by many small elven children throwing handfuls of petals before her bare feet. As they drew closer, the Queen nodded her head and gestured for the hunters to sit on chairs placed around the edge of the mirror pool, while the Queen occupied a large wooden throne highlighted with silver embellishments.

Fendi half stood in greeting, but Daeron laid a gentle hand on his arm and they waited in silence for the Queen to speak. Her voice was light but resonant, her words accompanied by the music of a harp. "Greetings travellers, I offer you comfort and rest after your long journey from the South Lands. Welcome Asher Grey of the mountain; Sir Varnon, of the plains; Baja and Raja of the mines; Daeron of the woods; and Randir, Fendi, Sienna and fairies of the South Lands. Welcome also to your companion, Violetta of Nnanell," and the purple-winged bird bowed its head as it perched on Randir's chair. The Queen continued, "It is with both pleasure and concern I meet and welcome you. I wish to discuss your travels shortly, but first we have other guests to introduce."

As the Queen stood again, Fendi couldn't help but admire her, for she appeared to glow from within, surrounded by a nimbus of soft white light. Her clothes were spun from the finest silk and covered in intricate embroidery that sparkled when she moved. She wore a crown with a glittering star on her head, atop long golden hair.

Fendi's gaze then shifted to the interesting assortment of beings entering the room via a curved staircase. The royal herald called out each name as they arrived. First were Harf and Gar of the mountain goblins, Fendi jumped up and clapped the small green creatures' filthy hands with glee. Next were Sir Brivan and Sir Philip of the Diagro knights whom Sir Varnon greeted with firm handshakes and smiles. Then two handsome brown centaurs who they had not met before who were introduced as Auriga and Baham.

Two dark haired mountain men named Garass Black and Mikel Brown sat as far away from the knights as possible. The black-eyed one glared unpleasantly at Asher, who appeared disappointed that they had not come to greet him. The shorter man, with hazel eyes, appeared quite uncomfortable, glancing nervously from one to the other.

Last to enter were Field Marshall Danir and his first soldier, Takskah of Diamond City, who were greeted with bellows of delight and thumps on the back from Baja and Raja. Baja had a quiet word with one of the elves and soon delicate glasses filled with honey mead were brought forth for the ever-thirsty dwarves. A gleeful smile lit up Baja's hairy face.

Introductions were made by the elven herald and a host of elven children brought around trays of delicate rice cakes and edible flowers for the delegates. There was much general discussion and talk of politics in the separate groups, so the halflings drifted off to one side, for such conversations had little meaning for them. Much to their surprise, Queen Liara-Star approached, shaking not only the halfling's hands, but also those of their tiny fairies.

Speaking in her resonant voice, the Queen addressed them, "We are in your debt, young halflings. We have learned that it was you who discovered the Vergai invaders in the South Lands and set off on a dangerous quest to protect the Elven Jewel."

Fendi looked crestfallen that the Queen had learned of their failure to warn Lakehaven, and the eventual capture of her niece, Princess Shari-Rose. "We are deeply sorry, your Majesty. We tried our best to save the princess for you." Fendi looked close to tears and she gave him a gentle pat on the arm.

"Your courage and determination have saved the South Lands from the Vergai invasion. I wish to offer you my thanks for your service to all our peoples. I would like you and Randir to relate your journey to us, so we can plan for the battle in the West Lands. I sometimes have the gift of visions and have seen a large horde coming through a dark portal." The halflings felt humbled by the praise but a little intimidated at the thought of addressing the large gathering.

The Queen bade everyone sit, before gesturing politely for Fendi to speak. The halfling recounted their adventures, aided here and there by Randir, when he forgot an important event, and they made sure to credit each of the hunters for their part in the journey. There was both praise and amazement when he described the kidnapping of the Princess and the battle of Bamber's Brook. He spoke of the underwater city and how the mermaids were on their way to help.

When he mentioned King Alpheratz sending centaurs to the West Lands, the centaurs raised their arms. Next Fendi described how they'd been taken to Desolate Castle where Violetta had sent lightning bolts through the portal. The wizard's apprentice promptly shape-shifted and stood to speak, but the elven Queen silenced her with a gesture. Violetta sat down, still beaming happily at being mentioned in the wonderful tale.

Fendi spoke of Wizard Nnald still performing the daily shield spell. The Queen had a doting smile at the mention of her old friend. Fendi's story ended with Heikki's flying machine and their flight across the desert and grasslands. The gnome gave a small bow and resumed his seat.

A buzz of excitement echoed around the throne room, but the Queen stood, silencing everyone with a gesture before detailing their plan. "The first order of business must be an alliance of all Relorians," she said in her gentle voice. There were angry looks between the knights and mountain men, but the knights reluctantly agreed since Sir Varnon and Asher were sitting side-by-side. Garass Black continued to glare at Asher and did not respond to the Queen.

Liara-Star continued, "Next we need a plan for battle in the west to include our new allies: the dwarves, centaurs, goblins and even mermaids. I will leave these preparations to Sir Philip and Garass Black, the emissary of the mountain men. For our alliance to succeed, you must convince your peoples to work together." Her gaze lingered briefly on the reluctant Garass, before she turned her attention to Asher.

"Asher Grey, you have led the Hunters of Reloria to victory in the South Lands and in the desert. I believe Fendi and Randir said that you have been charged by the Ancient Oracle to travel to Vergash and rescue Princess Shari-Rose." A wave of emotion crossed the elf Queen's delicate face, but she quickly regained her composure. "Shari-Rose is my niece and second in line to the elven throne. I am anxious to see her rescued.

147

We must also restore our protective shield if we are to repel both the Vergai, and now giants. It is very concerning that Daeron has had a vision of giants coming here, for they've not set foot in Reloria before. Their powers seem overwhelming so they must be stopped if our people are to survive.

"I wonder, Daeron, if I could try to link with your visions to see how Shari-Rose is faring in Vergash?" The elven guard was most honoured and knelt beside the Queen who took his hand and brought him to his feet. Closing her eyes in concentration, Cassie-Belle took her other hand. Suddenly all three gave a gasp, opening their eyes to gaze down into the pool.

The silvery reflection on the pool had been replaced by a vision of the elven princess being roughly yanked to her feet by a one-eyed giant. They glimpsed a fleeting image of Shari-Rose as she passed a mirror.

The Princess looked well and a clean white dress covered her Elven Jewel. Her hair was neatly combed and a puzzled look was on her beautiful face, but the question was answered when the long corridors she travelled ended in a large throne room.

Shari-Rose gasped and almost fainted, for lying on the floor of the Ar'gon Tower was her father, Crown-Prince

Celdar-Moon, surrounded by three giants. Emperor Chi'garu smiled malevolently while he studied the look of horror on her face. The Princess dropped to her knees, as though they gave way underneath her and she cradled her father's lifeless head in her hands, studying the dark brown scar across his forehead where the large half-pearl was blackened. She beat her hands on his still chest and cried out, "Father, Father, wake up!"

"Is he really your father?" asked the giant Emperor in amusement. "Well this really is just too much excitement. I thought you might have known him, but never guessed you'd be related. You know, young elf; it seems his elven jewel is just as powerless against me as yours. Ha ha ha."

The giant's laugh was echoed by his cronies as Shari-Rose wept bitterly on her father's chest. Her sobbing subsided a few minutes later when she realised that his chest was moving in long shallow breaths. "He's alive," she cried with joy, tears streaming down her face.

"Not for long," growled the Emperor wickedly. "Give me one good reason to keep this worthless elf alive, or I will kill him right now. I have no need for two hostages to persuade the elves to join Zanarah. I am sure you will be sufficient motivation." His hazel eye started to cloud over in transition to the deadly beam.

149

Shari-Rose stepped in front of her father, declaring bravely, "You will have to kill me first before you harm a hair on my father's head. He is heir to the elven throne of Reloria and is the closest thing you will ever see to the elven Queen. We will never join you!" She was trembling with fear and anger and her heart was pounding so hard she thought it would burst. To her great relief, the Cyclops paused and his eye slowly changed back to hazel.

"Ah, finally some fight in you, little elf. Well, I think it will amuse me for now to keep your father alive and if I have to kill your Queen, then I will still have the two heirs under my control. I do sense that you are the more dangerous one to my mission, so I'll keep you locked up here in the Ar'gon Tower with Master Ab'hijit to guard you." Chi'garu pointed towards a Cyclops who lounged on the stone bench looking possessively at the young princess. Shari-Rose felt a wave of fear at her new jailer's intense gaze.

Chi'garu appeared not to notice their exchange and continued, "I grow weary of this game. Take her away and send word to the battleships that I have decided to come and lead them to victory over Reloria myself. Go now and soften them up, Ga'hiji. Where are those pitiful wizards? Tell them I need a portal, now!" Shari-

Rose watched the Emperor march imperiously from the room.

General Ga'hiji followed behind muttering, "The ships could have gone through now, with the shield in tatters. Now they'll have to wait for him to come and command them. At least I get to go first, myself. I quite fancy having a castle there with lands and servants."

The Princess had one last look at her injured father before two giant guards dragged her struggling from the room.

"I can walk, you big buffoon!" said the Princess angrily, as the giants tossed her onto a large bed and left without a word. The Princess fumed and pounded the door in vain.

Back in Conlaoch Diarmada, the Queen concentrated harder, her hand touching the glittering star in her crown. The star burst into bright light and the Queen spoke urgently to the reflection in the pool, "Shari-Rose, can you hear me?" The princess's image didn't respond so the Queen gestured to Violetta and the three fairies, "Young apprentice, fairies, can you help me?"

Vi's face beamed with delight at the Queen's request. "I'd be honoured, your Majesty." The tiny fairies joined hands with her and the Queen in a circle of magic. "I have heard that fairies can amplify magic, but I have never seen it done. This is fantastic!" With iridescent wings beating quickly, the fairies sang, glowing like white hot fire as they amplified the magic. Violetta's white wand glowed too, as she uttered an enchantment. The air hummed and wavered, as the Queen spoke again, "Shari-Rose, can you hear me?"

Back in the Ar'gon Tower, the young Princess looked up when she heard the Queen. "Oh my goodness. Aunt Liara. Yes, I see you and Daeron and a small wizard holding your hand." The Princess tried to grab hold of them, but her fingers went straight through the image. Tears of frustration sprang from her green eyes. "Oh Aunty, it's dreadful. My Father has just been brought here, so that means the western shield has fallen. With the two most powerful shield keepers here, the shield will not protect you from the giants and the Vergai. They are coming through a portal and in battleships to invade Reloria. What can we do?"

"It is alright, dear one," replied the Queen. "Armies are coming from all over Reloria to fight these villains. There is also a group of hunters coming to rescue you in Vergash. Now, are you able to tell us where this Ar'gon Tower is located?"

With a heavy sigh, the princess replied, "You won't believe this aunt. It is so much worse than you imagine. I will have to show it to you. Come with me." Shari-Rose walked over to the window and the apparitions of the Queen, Daeron and Violetta went with her. She climbed up on a giant-sized chair and looked out the long slitted window. The companions could see an orange sky with a planet large in their view. "Look closely at the planet Aunt Liara. It is not the orange planet of Zanarah you see. It is a planet with large blue oceans and green forests. I believe I am looking at you on the planet of Zumar."

There were cries of surprise and alarm at the council meeting back on the world of Zumar. Everyone seemed to be speaking at once:

"That's impossible!"

"That cannot be Zanarah."

"What dat?"

"They're on another planet. It's incredible!"

"I don't believe it."

The meeting erupted into chaos and the elven herald had to rap his knuckles on his wooden chair to restore order. It took several minutes for the council to be seated and quiet once again.

The Queen and Violetta were still surrounded by the haze of magic and their reflection appeared in the pool below, next to the Princess on Zanarah. The Queen was trembling and Daeron had to help her stand upright to prevent her collapsing into the vision pool.

She spoke to her niece in a shaky voice, "Shari-Rose my dear. The magic is weakening. We will try to contact you again soon, but know that Daeron has a strong bond with you. He has seen you many times since you have been kidnapped. Know that you are not alone and we will find you, my dear......somehow." This last was said with despair, for though the Queen wanted to convince Shari-Rose; deep-down she did not believe it herself.

The images of the Queen, the guardian and the wizard's apprentice vanished from the pool, but the vision of the Princess lingered a few moments more and then that was gone as well. The elven Queen had turned as white as a sheet and now collapsed to the ground in a faint.

The conversations faltered at the sight of the Queen's strength being reduced to such a state. When she regained consciousness, Daeron, Vi and the guards escorted her from the throne room.

Fendi had been trying to make himself be heard above the babble of many agitated voices. Eventually he gave up yelling and Sienna put two fingers in her mouth and let out a shrill whistle, commanding abrupt silence.

"That's better," declared the young huntress. "Our negotiator has something important to say and you all need to hear it." She sat down next to Fendi, who looked a little surprised and stood up straight, to his full height of just past Asher's waist. Sienna could not help admiring the young halfling, his muscles now strong under the thin farm shirt he wore, shoulders growing broader and his face maturing week by week. She gave him a smile of encouragement.

Fendi addressed the gathering, "Please, we really need to establish our priorities. Sir Philip and Garass Black need to start work on the battle plans. We must assume that there is still an open portal on the western outpost, so perhaps we should send soldiers there, or we can go in Heikki's flying machine. I'll get the herald to write a treaty for you all to sign, so there will be no misunderstandings between races. Lastly, we need to find out if the wizard's apprentice has any idea what to do about making a portal to the planet of Zanarah or perhaps we need to speak to other Nnanell wizards."

Fendi then went about, dividing the council into practical groups to work on the different problems. Asher joined him and they spoke to Garass Black, Asher's countryman from Flame Mountain. The leader was tall like Asher with the same black hair and also a short, dark beard. He stood up from his conversation with Mikel Brown as Asher approached.

"I will not negotiate with this traitor and wife-stealer!" he declared and threw down a leather glove at Asher's feet.

Asher picked up the glove and handed it back to him. "I accept your challenge Garass and will happily fight you after this meeting has concluded. I have been working with the Diagro knights to defend Reloria against the Vergai invasion. That does not make me a traitor. Also I did not steal your wife while you were on your mission to the dwarves. She pursued me and I did not return her affections. Nevertheless, I would like to settle our disagreement as gentlemen and return to my people."

"You have no honour, no name and no one will recognise you," yelled Garass emphatically and spat at the ground near Asher's feet. He turned on his heel and stormed over to speak with the centaurs.

The brown haired man named Mikel Brown stood and spoke to Asher, "Please accept my apologies for his behaviour, friend Ash. I never believed Hydrane's accusations to be true. She has a fiery temper and couldn't bear your refusal to come to her while her husband was away. You were a strong man to resist her temptations and a stronger man still to leave your home when you were not in the wrong. He should admit he was wrong and get over it."

Asher gave a wry laugh, "A stubborn man like Garass admit he was wrong? It'll be a cold day on Flame Mountain when that happens. The best I hope for is to be allowed to return to my family in peace. I have no love for politics or other men's troublesome wives." Asher sighed and sat down next to his countryman. "Thanks for believing me Mik. You stood by me through the worst of it." Mikel looked at Asher with regret in his hazel eyes and clasped his shoulder firmly in friendship.

Garass stormed back towards them, black eyes blazing as he loudly declared, "You think you're too good for her. That's it, isn't it? You don't want the mountain women because you're better than us." Garass punched Asher squarely on the jaw, but Asher steeled himself and stood his ground. Garass reached for a wickedly sharp dagger from his belt, but Asher knocked the blade spinning into some ornamental bushes. Garass then grabbed Asher's leather collar and tried to drag him off down the marble staircase.

Asher tried to remain calmly detached and only defend against Garass, but his innate fighting skills kicked in. He blocked Garass with a solid upward thrust, followed by a roundhouse kick, sending him sprawling on the floor.

Garass retaliated with a kick to Asher's calf and with an inhuman roar launched himself on his countryman. The two men tumbled from view down the stairs and the beating of wings a minute later signalled them taking their fight to the sky.

Fendi sought a glimpse of their duel, but tall towers blocked his view, so he ran up a nearby tower, taking the long spiral staircase two steps at a time. He emerged into bright sunlight atop a viewing platform, closely followed by Randir and Sienna.

The mid-air fight was an amazing sight, with two dragons ducking and weaving in the air currents. Garass was a jet-black dragon, with onyx scales under his wings and slightly smaller than Ash Dragon, but he was a dirty fighter and dangerous opponent.

The dragons flew rapidly towards each other, before changing direction in the last second. The watchers held their breath. Many times it looked as though the massive creatures would collide, only to swiftly change direction again. Sharp talons reached out, attempting to injure each other and sending balls of flame hurtling through the air. One fire ball landed in the elven forest not far from the city, causing a flock of birds to flee the smoke.

Asher was the larger and stronger of the two, but Garass was enraged. They flew directly at each other. Neither gave way and crashed together in a sickening crunch of bone. Garass raked his sharp talons down Asher's right wing, tearing the thin membrane on the last fold. Asher gave a hoarse shriek of pain, blasting Garass with a fireball, the intensity of which propelled him far into the air.

By now, most of the council had joined the halflings on the rose towers and ooh'd and ahh'd with each violent encounter. The third shape-shifter, Mikel Brown then launched into the sky. Mik Dragon was only half the size of Garass and was brown with amber plates under his wings. He tried to position himself between injured

Ash and his attacker, but the black dragon enveloped the brown in a ball of fire. Mik Dragon frantically beat his wings trying to escape the searing heat.

Garass again swooped on Ash Dragon as he was testing his damaged wing, the strength of the black dragon's downward momentum forced the grey dragon crashing into a castle spire. Ash slid down the sloping marble before regaining his balance, then launched upwards with a powerful thrust of his wings. His barbed tail whipped out, stunning the black dragon's spiked head. Garass fell heavily towards the castle. He fell onto a pointed spire, ripping a gaping hole in his left wing, and, spinning rapidly before he crashed into a courtyard out of the sight below.

Mik Dragon and Ash flew down to the castle. The black dragon lay crumpled on the marble pavestones, slowly reverting back to human form as they watched. His left arm hung limp by his side and he cried out in pain and frustration. The other two dragons shimmered back to human form and went to his aid. Garass' eyes opened at their touch and he immediately tried to stand, but his left leg gave way underneath him, clearly broken. Some elves brought out a stretcher and he was carried away, yelling insults to Asher as he left.

Raja inspected Asher's arm and found the wrist was broken. He brought his pan pipes out of his pocket and played a soothing tune, quickly healing the broken bones. Asher gingerly bent his wrist this way and that to test it and gasped in surprise. "Why, it's as good as new, Raja. Amazing!" He gave the stocky dwarf a clap on the back in thanks and admiration.

Mikel Brown appeared uninjured and shook Asher's mended hand. "Ash, you know that **you** are meant to lead the mountain men, not Garass. It was probably Garass who put Hydrane up to the events which led to your exile. You are a much fairer leader and we would follow you, as we do your father. You must come back with me and help us prepare for the war with the Vergai."

Asher shook his head slowly, "I am bound to these hunters on a quest to rescue the Princess. I will come with you briefly to Flame Mountain, but then I must leave, for if we fail in our quest, the lands will be overrun by the Vergai, and now it seems, giants as well. These are even worse and have a burning ray which shines from their single eye. No, friend Mik, I must go and do my part wherever this quest takes us. If Garass will not lead our people, then I charge you to do it in my absence."

Mikel Brown bowed low before Asher and slowly rose to look his friend in the eye. "So be it, Asher Grey. We will ally with the Diagro knights to defend Reloria, and if Garass does not like it, he can remain on the mountain. We must get Hydrane to confess so the mountain men will follow your command. Of course getting her to back down will be a formidable challenge in its own right, but it must be done." Asher nodded in agreement and shook his friend's hand once more.

The hunters of Reloria gathered back around the vision pool. Sir Varnon was the first to speak, "So Ash, are we all going with you to Flame Mountain? I don't know if they would accept a knight there."

"I think getting the portal closed is our first priority," Asher replied, his yellow-green eyes blazing at the thought of battle. "Mikel and I will get reinforcements from Flame Mountain and meet you there. You can take the others in the gnome's flying machine. I will sign the treaty with the other leaders and take a copy of it to Flame Mountain, where I believe the men will follow me when they learn of the invasion. Garass Black can make his own decisions, whether or not to join us."

*   *   *

An hour later the treaty had been signed by the remaining parties and the hunters waited by the mirror pool for the Queen to come from her chambers.

Cassie-Belle and Daeron had returned a short time earlier. She was giving Daeron meaningful glances as they waited. He stoically avoided her gaze, but with a look of regret on his pale face. Fendi realised that while Lady Cassie-Belle and guardian Daeron had deep feelings for each other, it was not possible for them to be together due to elven customs. He guessed that here in the Elven Heart it would be more difficult for them to speak than in the isolated southern outpost. Then Fendi glanced at the beautiful huntress sitting next to him, carving arrows with a sturdy hunting knife, and marvelled at how love could bring unlikely people together.

He turned to Daeron, "Is it forbidden for a high elf and a common elf to be together?" he asked.

Daeron slowly turned his head away from studying Cassie-Belle's dainty elven features. "Well, not forbidden, but it is frowned upon. Usually high elves look down on us and would not be interested in us romantically. High elves are magic users and often have arranged marriages to keep the magic strong. Cassie-Belle is young and beautiful. I do not wish to see her throw her life away on a much older elf, who cannot give her the life to which she is entitled. I will spend my life in service to the royal family as a guardian, while she should marry and raise a family with her own kind. I wish only for her happiness."

Cassie-Belle walked quietly over to him and turned his face to look at her, "Daeron, do not be so modest. You are the most wonderful elf I have ever met and you have dedicated your life to guarding my friend, Shari-Rose. I can think of no other elf more worthy of my affections. I didn't realise I was in love with you until I was almost killed by the Vergai and I nearly lost you, so I promised myself that if I got you back, I would confess my feelings to you."

Daeron stroked her long brown hair, "I am flattered, my Lady, for you are the kindest and sweetest elf I have ever met. I have watched you grow into a beautiful young woman, who almost gave her life for her best friend. I am truly sorry that a romance would not be possible between us, and my hope is for you to find love with a high-born elf." He kissed her delicate hand, patted it and gave a small regretful sigh as he turned away. He did not see the look of despair in sweet Cassie-Belle's face, or the tears welling up in her eyes.

Changing the subject, Daeron spoke to the hunters, "Violetta says she knows the location of the wizard's stronghold and will take us there once the western portal is secure."

Violetta smiled when she heard her name, skirting around the pool to the elves and halflings. The wizard's apprentice had bathed and changed into a long black dress of elven design, with stars around the hem. She had done something strange with her raven hair and fashioned it in small knots with little ends of hair hanging down from each one. Now she fiddled nervously with her white wand, and the hunters smiled at the funny young lady with twinkling violet eyes.

"So. You want me to come with you then?" she asked happily.

"Well seeing as you are the only one who knows where we are going, it looks like you are our guide," remarked Asher pretending to be grumpy. He couldn't frown for long, for he was growing fond of the dimpled apprentice.

Baja and Raja had a quiet word between them and then Baja said, "Only if you can control your tongue. We don't want to wear earplugs the whole journey."

"I concur," agreed Sir Varnon. "Too much talking and you shall be a furmal for the entire voyage. Now, are you going to tell me where we are going?"

"I don't think that would be a good idea," countered Violetta. "If you know where we are going, then you may not need me to come. I'll let you know when we get there."

There were sighs from the hunters but their attention was diverted by the opening of the royal apartments. From the gleaming tower, the Queen emerged into the sunlight, looking as radiant as ever while elven children scattered petals at her feet. There was however, a slight heaviness to her gait and a slump in her delicate shoulders that had not been there before. It bordered on a look of defeat, as though the thought of losing her brother and niece was too much for her to bear.

The hunters respect for the elven ruler increased as she reached the council gathering, for she lifted her head high, straightened her back and addressed them with squared shoulders. "Fellow council members, I apologise for delaying you, for it is vital that we move in haste. The hunters of Reloria have been charged with rescuing Princess Shari-Rose and this quest must continue. There is a massive army gathering across the seas in Vergash intent on landing on our shores within two weeks.

"We have dwarves, mountain goblins and trolls here already and we gratefully accept their help. The centaurs are on their way and will arrive here in the next week, ready for battle. The knights of Diagro have pledged their assistance, as well as the mountain men, as soon as word can be sent to their homelands. I will prepare the elves for battle and we'll set forth for the western lands within two days.

"I thank-you for allying in the defence of Reloria and leave you now to your battle preparations. If there are any supplies or food you require, please ask my herald to assist you and so I bid you all a safe and successful journey. I would however, request a word alone with the hunters before you leave."

And so the delegates from each race paid their respects to the Queen as they left.

Fendi's goblin friend Gar and his father, Harf came to speak before they left. Fendi gave the little green goblins a friendly handshake, "Hello Gar and Harf. I hear you are leading the goblins and trolls to battle the Vergai at the western outpost."

Young Gar nodded with a sharp-toothed grin, still wearing the same dirty loincloth since Fendi first met him at the waterfall. "Me go stab stab bad Vergai. Bring big trolls to club club. You hurry to come Fendi. Not want to miss good fight and stab stab."

Fendi gave a little smile, "Yes Gar. We'll be there to help you as soon as we can, but our first priority is to close the portal and to rescue the Princess. I'm sure you'll do very well fighting the Vergai in our absence. This is only the start of the war, for we know that hundreds of ships are coming, and giants too. They will be extremely difficult to defeat, so we'll try to return as soon as possible to help you."

Harf held out his hand, "Good bye Fendi. We go and do good fight. We watch silly dwarves. They not smart." This last brought a laugh from all of the hunters, except feigned anger from the dwarven brothers.

Randir replied to the goblins, "Yes Harf. It would be good if you stay with the dwarves. Some of them are miners and just learning to fight, but you goblins and trolls are fierce fighters and I know you will fight bravely. Well, it is almost a week's travel, so we'll let you get started. Good luck."

The goblins shook hands with the hunters, waved to Heikki and Violetta, and left. Apparently the trolls had been causing some disruption among the elven community in the woods and Garf and Har were needed urgently.

Sir Philip and Sir Brivan of the Diagro knights also took their leave, departing north-west to the Diagro castles to marshal more knights for the coming battle. Preparations were also needed to defend the plains and coastline, for it had not yet been determined where the Vergai battleships were likely to attack. There were still almost eighty knights who had survived the long voyage to the Southlands, encamped in the elven forest near Conlaoch Diarmada with their squires, horses and hounds. Sir Varnon promised to visit them before breaking camp.

Queen Liara-Star clasped hands with each of the hunters as she addressed them. "I wish you good fortune my friends. Celdar-Moon is heir to my throne and his daughter is very important to Reloria. They are the only ones capable of merging the spells of the four shield-raisers together to create the Shield of Reloria, so our protection has gone. I wish I could come with you, but I know the Ancient Oracle has foreseen that you alone must fight the Vergai. This is a quest that only you can fulfil and I wish you all success. Please take care of my dear family. "

The elf, with tears welling in her big blue eyes, embraced each hunter. Violetta surprised her with an exuberant hug, telling her they would not rest until the missing elves were brought home.

The hunters were again given pixie flowers and floated down to the evergreen forest. Out of sight on top of the tower, the Queen nervously watched their departure, hoping for a miracle to save them all from destruction.

CHAPTER 8 : FLAME MOUNTAIN

At the edge of the clearing, Cassie-Belle was waiting amid the blossoming trees. "Daeron, may I say goodbye before you leave?" she asked politely.

"Of course, my Lady," he replied and offered her his arm. Cassie-Belle smiled and placed her hand on his. They walked a short way from the others, where Sir Varnon was busily giving instructions to knights gathered with their squires, horses and dogs.

Daeron nimbly ducked behind a flowering tree and Cassie-Belle pulled him into a gentle embrace. "Daeron, you are coming back aren't you? I just couldn't bear to lose you as well as the Princess. I think my heart would break completely."

Daeron clasped her pale hands to his heart and earnestly replied, "There is no place I'd rather be than wherever you are. Please don't fret for it would make me worry about you. I do promise to return to you, and if it is possible to travel to Zanarah and back, then I will be bringing your best friend and her father with me."

Cassie-Belle looked shyly at him, "Daeron, would you do me a favour and wear this locket for me. It would comfort me to know that you have something of mine to remember me by." She handed Daeron a delicate silver locket containing a lock of her hair.

"You are too modest," he replied. "I could never forget you, no matter how far or how long I travel to rescue Shari-Rose. The memory of your sweet smile will stay in my mind forever." He picked a nearby blossom and handed it to her, then gently touched the delicate tips of her pointed ears, with a sigh of regret. Cassie-Belle fastened the locket's chain around his neck and before he could go, she kissed him deeply.

"Come back to me," she whispered and quickly ran off into the dappled light of the elven forest.

*   *   *

Mikel Brown was waiting for the hunters at the edge of the clearing. He spoke directly to Asher, "Come friend

Ash, we'd best fly to Flame Mountain to gather what help we can to recapture the outpost."

Asher nodded and gestured to Daeron, as he appeared from the woods, "Come elf, I may need your help to convince the Flame Mountain Council of the urgency of our mission." Daeron gave a small bow of acceptance and followed the tall mountain man.

The hunters watched the two mountain men shimmer into the mighty dragons. Ash Dragon towered above the trees, his wings folded over emerald scales. Mik Dragon was dwarfed by his larger friend, but was no less impressive, his amber eyes and scales gleaming in a brown body.

Fendi ran over to Ash Dragon and called up to him, "Ash, take me with you please."

The dragon stared down at him, and was about to respond when Sienna called out, "If he goes, I go too." The huntress had a stubborn look in her big brown eyes and Ash Dragon gave a very human-sounding sigh of resignation.

Speaking in his deep dragon's voice, he said, "Come if you must, young halflings. Make sure you find a comfortable place on my back and hold on tight. It be a long way to the ground if you fall."

Randir shook his head in disbelief as Fendi and Sienna climbed high on the dragon's back. They found a spot at the base of his long neck, where they squeezed between the spines. Sienna held Fendi tightly around the waist and he leaned back a little into her comforting arms. Lashing a rope around the dragon's neck he secured them both to the dragon for safety and their fairies held tightly to the dragon spines with their halflings.

Bossy Randir-La called out to them, "You're crazy! Do you have any idea how fast a dragon can fly?" She looked quite concerned for her fairy friends.

Fendi gave a nervous laugh and called back, "I expect we're about to find out, but I'm curious to see where the mountain men live. It's a once-in-a-lifetime opportunity."

"We'll race you to the western outpost," called Randir, as he backed away from the large dragons. "I'll try to save a few Vergai for you."

With a snort, Ash Dragon beat his wings creating great gusts of wind in the clearing and leaped into the air with

Fendi and Sienna hanging on for dear life. Daeron rode on Mik Dragon, in the graceful way that only an elf can. The dragons accelerated, leaving the elven forest far below them, and the halflings screamed, though whether with fright or exhilaration they weren't quite sure.

A deep, throaty chuckle was coming from Ash Dragon. "I could fly upside down if it's a thrill you're after," he chortled in his deep voice.

Fendi gasped in fright, "No Asher, no! This is more than enough excitement, but thanks anyway," he shouted, knuckles white as he tightened his grip on the rope. Ash Dragon laughed again, accelerating rapidly toward the sunset, and Mik Dragon had to flap his smaller wings almost twice as fast to keep up with the huge grey.

Twilight came. The two bond-fairies huddled together in Fendi's lap, with arms around each other.

Sienna rested her head against Fendi's warm shoulder and was soon asleep while Fendi watched the stars come out. Their twin planet Zanarah was visible overhead with its moon shining brightly. He could see the orange patterns of the planet and wondered about the strange place Shari-Rose was held captive.

*   *   *

As daybreak came, Fendi woke, trying to stretch a little and regain some feeling in his numb, cold toes. The air was very cool and the halflings cuddled tightly together for warmth. "Are you awake?" Fendi whispered over his shoulder to Sienna.

"Almost," she replied and he could feel her cheek stretching into a smile as she leaned around him for a kiss. She ran her fingers through his shoulder-length brown curls. "Your hair is getting long, you know. I wonder if Ash Dragon flies whilst he's asleep, or if he's been awake the entire night. He must be exhausted."

The dragon turned his large grey head to look sideways at the halflings. "We can half-sleep, like some animals, but I will need a rest when we finally get there. Mik Dragon is slowing down and I think perhaps we might have to stop and let him sleep for a while." The halflings turned to look at the smaller brown dragon who was flying low behind them over rolling black hills which were turning into a craggy black mountain range.

Ash Dragon called out to his companion, "Come on Mik. We have reached the Black Foothills. Let's find a cave and sleep for a while." The two dragons descended lower over the craggy mountains and Ash's keen eyes soon located a cave in the side of a broken off peak. Landing on mountain top, the two dragons reverted to human form and climbed down the steep cliff face with the aid of Fendi's stout rope.

"These mountains are strange," remarked Sienna, as they abseiled down the cliff to the cave entrance. "I have never seen such bare soil, so little plant-life and barely any trees for miles. Did something happen here?"

"We are getting towards mountain men country now," Mikel answered her. The soil here is black from the volcanoes, but contains a strange substance which prevents many plants from growing here. There are a few farms near Flame Mountain growing root vegetables, but most of us prefer to live just on meat. Dragons weren't meant to be vegetarians."

"How far is it to Flame Mountain?" asked Fendi. "I'm looking forward to seeing where you live."

"I don't know what the welcome will be like," said Asher despondently. "I left in rather a hurry after a big fight

177

with Garass which I lost rather badly. I was too surprised and hurt by his wife's accusations to defend myself. I didn't make the same mistake yesterday. I tried not to injure him, but he was determined to kill me, so I had to fight back. I didn't intend for him to break his leg in the fall, but I think that he will be even angrier when he is able to fly again and come after me. I know his pride won't let him drop the issue, even if he's proven wrong."

Eventually they were all on the tiny ledge at the cave entrance. Asher went into the cave first, to check that it was safe. "Come on in. This cave has been abandoned for a long time. There are few animals nearby for there's little vegetation to support life and they have been hunted almost to extinction anyway. We have to range farther and farther afield to find food. The Diagro Plains in contrast are an abundant food source, which is the reason for the constant disputes."

They followed Asher into the low-roofed cave, which extended a fair way back into darkness. The glowing fairies provided some illumination, revealing worn blankets and bones scattered in several places around the floor. The remains of a campfire were to one side inside the cave entrance.

Fendi-La looked rather worried and whispered to Asher, "Ash, I think that someone may be coming back here and we should leave."

"Don't worry little one," the large mountain man replied with a smile. He was stooped over in the confined cave and gave the fairy a reassuring pat, which was surprisingly gentle despite his large, calloused hands. "This is a cave of mine, which I use from time to time when I seek solitude. I haven't been here for many months and I don't think anyone else comes here. There are hundreds of caves closer to Flame Mountain for the mountain people to occupy."

The fairy looked with a frown at the messy state of his cave, "Well Ash, it certainly could use a bit of a woman's touch." She directed them to pile up the bones neatly in a corner, to make space for them to sleep. Once the cave was tidied to Fendi-La's satisfaction, they all lay down on their bedrolls.

Young Mikel was asleep and snoring gently within minutes and Asher tucked a worn blanket around his shoulders, with a fatherly smile, while Daeron hummed in a low tone, as he oiled his leather belt. He passed the small jar of oil to Asher and they sat contentedly cleaning the dust from their leather, while Sienna whittled arrows, as she often did in the evening. Asher lit a small fire near the entrance of the cave, and the smoke drifted out into the sunny sky.

Asher spoke to Daeron in a low murmur, "I'm worried that by the time we gather the dragons and close this portal that there'll be swarms of Vergai and giants all over the western plains. I don't even know if the dragons will come with me after they banished me in disgrace. I'm not exactly their most trusted warrior anymore. That honour rests with Garass, who will do probably anything to stop me after our meeting in the elven kingdom."

Daeron thought carefully before replying, studying the hilt of his sword as he spoke, "I had dealings with the men of Flame Mountain many decades ago when I was assigned to the western outpost, before the princess was born. In general I have found the mountain men to be fair and just, respecting and obeying their counsel leaders. They do have one fault that I am aware of..." The elf then looked directly into Asher's eyes, "They are invariably stubborn and difficult to reason with when they have an idea set their mind. Look at your history with the Diagro knights: centuries of war, and slaying all the peace emissaries the knights have sent. Surely you have learnt something of the knights' character from your friendship with Lord Varnon."

Asher ran his fingers roughly through his short, dark hair and gave a growl. "Then expect a warm welcome when we get there, elf. We'll be lucky if they don't fry us before we can speak to them."

Fendi raised his hands in a gesture of peace, "Calm now friends. We're weary and need a rest. This can wait until later. I'm sure between us, we'll figure out the best way to convince your council. The mountain men will realise the truth of the invasion sooner or later and I think the sooner the better, for us all."

Sienna gave Fendi a pat on the back for his wise words that defused the tension in the cave. Fendi-La also gave him a smile and holding hands with Sienna-Li, broke into a rendition of 'Rest, ye weary traveller."

Fendi and Sienna watched the fairies sing and dance their bedtime ritual, their aches and cares melting away with the gentle music. Fendi wrapped his arms around the huntress and she snuggled her head into his chest. "Sleep well, sweet huntress," he whispered into her tangled hair. She replied with a satisfied sigh and cuddled even closer.

*   *   *

They slept for several hours in the cave. Sienna was the first to wake and due to her hunter instincts, was instantly alert.   Fendi's arm was still around her, resting gently on her abdomen. She had slipped off her clothes when they were under the blanket and lay only in her undershirt.

Glancing around the dark cave she saw the slight glow of the fairies a short distance from her, curled up together on their large red and white toadstools. Towards the back of the cave were three more sleeping figures, Daeron, Asher and Mikel breathing heavily in their sleep.

Sienna tried to roll over and view the rest of the cave to check for any danger, but as she moved, Fendi half woke, his hand moving from her abdomen to the curve of her hip. He caressed her smooth skin in his sleep and gave a low, happy moan. Sienna felt a strange feeling, like butterflies in her stomach and stopped rolling, uncertain what to do next. She took slow deep breaths to calm herself, for the wave of unfamiliar emotions made her heart beat rapidly, and her lips tingle.

Rolling over she wrapped her arms firmly around his shoulders and kissed him deeply. He sat up and pulled her onto his lap, kissing her all the while. One strong arm wrapped snuggly around her slim shoulders and the other hand gently stroked her soft brown cheek, and she gave a low murmur of contentment at his touch. When Fendi's hand gently moved down her side to her waist, she realised that she was only in her undershirt, so with a final kiss she gently pulled away from him to dress.

Fendi sighed and whispered, "I love you, my sweet Sienna. I hope that one day we can spend some time alone together. Perhaps we could go back to those beautiful waterfalls at Baretop Mountains. That was such a romantic place. I just want to hold you forever and never let go." He stroked her long brown hair tumbling down around her singlet.

She dressed quickly before giving him another long kiss. "I love you too, dear Fendi, and I'm so glad I'm sharing these adventures with you, for we never know where we'll be or what will happen from one day to the next. If you'd told me two days ago that I would be riding a dragon to Flame Mountain, I would never have believed it."

Fendi nodded in agreement and stretched his arms up high. Sienna noticed with appreciation the muscled definition in his bare chest from his daily sword practice with Sir Varnon and gave a little sigh as he pulled his shirt over his head. Rummaging in his backpack, Fendi found some elven bread to share with her. "I hope the mountain men will have a decent meal for us," he said. Sienna agreed, for though the bread was soft and filled the stomach, it did not compare with having something warm in their bellies.

They shared their food with Asher, Mikel and Daeron when they woke, and Mikel thanked them, remarking, "I think I'll keep an eye out for mountain goats as we fly today. I could use some meat in my belly. The elven food is nice, but not very satisfying. I don't think my flame would last on such a diet."

Asher nodded too and gave a harrumph. "Elves and centaurs don't eat any meat. It's a wonder you have any strength at all, Daeron." The elf shrugged his shoulders and Asher continued, "Well, the daylight's passing. We'd best get to Flame Mountain before dusk. Who knows what our reception will be like without Garass? Halflings, to save you climbing all the way back up the cliff, I'll jump out the entrance to transform, then hover just below the ledge, so you can jump on my back."

Fendi's eyes widened, "Are you sure that's safe Asher?"

"I won't let you fall," replied the mountain man, crouching under the low ceiling. The halflings gave cries of fright, as he dove straight from the tunnel entrance and down the cliff. A few seconds later, they heard the beat of massive wings and a huge gust of air filled the cave when he came into view.

The halflings shouldered their small backpacks and bedrolls, then Sienna was brave enough to leap first. "Here I come, Ash," she called as she leapt towards Ash Dragon, still trying to coordinate his flying to hover just below the entrance. She landed on the base of the dragon's neck and caught the rope that Fendi threw to her and tied it on.

Following her, Fendi landed painfully on one of the dragon's large spines, grunting with discomfort, then grabbed on to Sienna to save himself from sliding down Ash's back. She helped him up behind her and they tied the rope tightly around each other, sighing with relief as the dragon moved away from the cave to give Mikel room for his jump.

The smaller mountain man looked nervously at the view below the cave, a steep drop onto jagged rocks, leaving little room for error. Running his fingers through his brown hair and with a fearful look in his eyes, he took a few steps backward and came dashing out of the cave in a stooped run, jumping high into the air. He plummeted towards the rocks below and the fairies cried out in fright as he fell quickly, transforming himself just a few feet from the ground. Frantically beating his wings, he managed to arrest his fall in the nick of time. Halflings and fairies cheered with relief while the dragons screeched loudly.

Mik Dragon flew up to the ledge and Daeron nimbly leapt across the gap, then the brown dragon drew alongside Ash and they flew west towards Flame Mountain.

The four hours to their homelands passed quickly, with plenty to see along the way. The black ground was covered with straggly grass in places and families of mountain goats sought cover when they detected the dragons overhead.

The terrain grew higher and craggier as they approached Flame Mountain and the sky was alive with dragons flying singly and in groups of two or three. The beasts' colour and size ranged from the large black or grey, to the medium-sized brown and green, and small red and maroon ones about the size of a human which Ash called wyverns.

These wyverns were not unlike miniature dragons, but without front limbs and their tails had a poisonous barb on the end, which resulted in sudden death if they pierced the skin. Wyverns tended to stay among their own kind and lived closer to the base of the mountains in packs of five to eight. Ash explained that they could not breathe fire and were considered an inferior species by some of the larger dragons.

The halflings and their fairies marvelled at this strange land of mythical beasts come to life. "I had always thought that dragons were imaginary creatures my father invented to scare me into behaving as a young boy," Fendi confessed to the dragons. "I would have never believed this sight in a million years." He ducked instinctively as a group of three green dragons flew over them, golden scales under their wings were gleaming in the bright sunlight.

Fendi studied the mighty beasts flying. "Ash, I've noticed that dragons tend to have their last name as their colour. You called Garass Black's partner Hydrane Blue. Does that mean that there are blue dragons as well?"

The dragon gave a very human-looking scowl at the mention of Garass and Hydrane. "Hopefully we won't see her, but knowing her meddling ways, she will come to us. Yes, she is blue, although different to these dragons you see here. I'd best warn you before we get there that Hydrane is a Hydra, which is related to a dragon, but prefers to live in the water. They are blue or purple and are born with two heads. If one head is cut off, two more will grow in its place. The hydras are untrustworthy and often pick quarrels with the dragons to amuse themselves. The grey dragons want to rid Reloria of these malicious creatures, but the black dragons stick up for them. It is a bone of contention between our clans."

"This one, Hydrane, is the worst of the lot. She uses her feminine wiles to cause friction between the dragons and she is not content with having Garass Black. She wants to add other male dragons to her list of conquests. I think that Garass is a fool for falling in love with her and then leaving her when he goes away on missions. I have seen her getting up to mischief with other black dragons and last year she tried it on me as well. She had half the clans believing that I was a slave to her beauty and blindly obeying her commands. I left the mountain, rather than face the humiliation. So, no, Fendi, I do not wish to see the hydras."

Ash Dragon grew quite sombre after this and they flew on in silence toward a towering volcano rising well above the surrounding mountain range, and halfway up its steep side was a plateau with a blue lake.

The dragons' wings beat strongly as they ascended through a cloud of white smoke. Looking down, they saw red-hot molten lava bubbling and sizzling in the crater and flowing in a river down one side. Waves of heat enveloped them as they flew up through the lowest clouds to gaze at this incredible sight. Ears' popping with the change in air pressure, they also found it hard to breathe in the thin air and were more than thankful when the dragons returned to the plateau by the lake.

A number of black stone structures were built around the lake, unnoticed by Fendi during their ascent. "This is our high assembly," explained Ash Dragon, landing gently near the tall buildings with peaked roofs and many rounded pillars on each side. The dragon could have easily fit inside its enormous doorway, but as soon as the halflings slid down his scaly back, he returned to being a mountain man.

"It is customary to be in human form while on the ground," Asher explained. His friend Mikel had also shape-shifted and was standing close beside him. As the halflings got their bearings, other dragons landed around them and changed to human form.

189

"Don't go too near the lake," Ash warned as the halflings looked into the shadowy depths. "The untrustworthy hydras live there and would drown you for their own sport." Fendi and Sienna stepped back quickly.

Asher led the way into the assembly building with a crowd of mountain men following. There was no welcome or discussion, just an air of expectation from the silent crowd, and the halflings looked worriedly at the stern faces.

Inside the building, they walked past statues of men and dragons along both sides of the long hall. The statues were made of polished black stone. Fendi and Sienna admired the intricate detail in the carvings, and it almost seemed they might spring into life at any second. Each pair of statues was in an alcove between supporting columns with candles flickering at the foot of each one in a gesture of tribute and respect.

At the end of the long hall on a raised dais were seven occupied chairs, the centre chair being somewhat higher than the others. Asher spoke quietly, "The Flame Mountain Council and the President, Aram Grey. He is my father, but I won't get any preferential treatment from him. He is wise and just and will review the matter on its own merits. There is a council member from each of the six dragon and wyvern clans and Garass' Uncle Ember is the black clan representative. I believe he will try to be impartial, but his loyalty may be affected when he realises that Garass' name is absent from the treaty document. Have patience my friends, for this debate may take a while."

They approached the raised dais and Asher, Mikel and Daeron bowed before the council. The halflings thought it prudent to do the same. The council members were uniformly white-haired with five men and two women on the dais, dressed in a variety of leather garments that gave the impression of a people constantly at war. They looked sternly at Asher and it was his father who addressed them first, "What is the meaning of this intrusion, Asher?" His tone was angry and his yellow-green eyes bore in Asher's.

Asher bowed low again and his voice rang strong and clear in the large forum. "Greetings President Aram Grey and councillors, I bring before you two halflings from the Southlands, who have news of a new Vergai invasion of our lands.   This is Fendi of Southdale and Sienna the huntress from the Wild Woods. Also here is Daeron, an elf from the southern elven outpost who witnessed the attack." The elf and halflings bowed low again and Fendi took a nervous step towards the stony-faced councillors.

He tried to calm himself with deep breaths and the thought of all the other races he had helped to ally during their quest. "I can do this," he thought to himself, squaring his shoulders and standing as tall as he could to waist-height among the tall humans.

"I am Fendi, son of Fandri and I have fought with Asher and Daeron against Vergai in the Zanzi Grasslands of the south, and the Great Eastern Desert. I bring news from the elves of Conlaoch Diarmada that the Vergai have invaded the West Lands and thousands more are travelling here in ships from Vergash. They bring giants with them and seek to destroy all the good peoples of Reloria. Here is the alliance treaty which has been signed by seven races of Relorians." Asher gave it to his father.

President Aram Grey studied the document and passed it to the councillors, who each read it carefully and passed it on. There were low mutters of disapproval from the council.

Then the President stood before the large assembly now filling the forum. He wore heavy golden chains of office around his neck, his white hair was short and spiked like Asher's and one could see a distinct resemblance between the two. However, Aram's face held none of Asher's laughter lines and his eyes were colder and harder. "This treaty was signed by Mikel Brown. Where is Garass Black who was sent to the elves as our ambassador? Why is his name not on the treaty and why did he not deliver it to me himself?" He waved the document towards Asher and his voice was icy with anger.

Asher gestured to Fendi that he would respond himself, "Garass refused to sign the treaty because the Diagro knights are part of the alliance. But I believe this invasion must take precedence over our war with the knights and that if we do not join the alliance, then Reloria will fall. I have seen these Vergai in action and they have slaughtered entire villages including women and children. They are not here to conquer; they are here to obliterate us!" Asher's eyes flashed with anger, but he reined his emotions in to meekly step back, waiting for the council to respond.

Ember Black called out, "How can you trust the word of this man. He took the wife of another and fled our lands in disgrace?" There was a murmur of assent amongst the council.

Another councillor stood, "This is hearsay and conjecture, not fact. Asher left before the matter could be investigated. I suggest we concentrate on the issue at hand and leave this man's reputation for another time." Asher nodded and bowed his head towards the man.

There was a commotion at the back of the great hall and indignant cries as members of the congregation were rudely pushed aside. The mountain men gave a wide berth to this intruder and drew back against the walls. Fendi-La gave a gasp when she saw the woman causing the ruckus.

She was a bizarre sight indeed. She was tall and solidly built, with two heads on overly-long necks sprouting from her broad shoulders. Her hair was black and hung down her back from both heads, though her facial features were rather plain, apart from her startling silver eyes.

She scrutinised the crowd as though looking for someone and when she caught sight of Asher, she ran to him and slapped him hard across the left cheek. The slap caught the mountain man by surprise, but his quick reflexes kicked in and he grabbed onto her hand. The two-headed woman collapsed against him and threw her free arm around him. She cried from both her mouths at once, "Oh Asher, Asher, how could you leave me like that? You know I love you and would go with you to the ends of Reloria." The woman's words startled the halflings and the huge room was so quiet you could have heard a pin drop.

The silence was broken by the stern voice of President Aram Grey. "Hydrane Blue; you appear to have deceived our people with your accusations that Asher thrust his unwanted attentions on you, in fact it seems that is exactly what you are trying to do to him. Have you no respect for your marriage to Garass Black?" A look of disgust was clear on the leader's face. "Go, tend to your eggs before they are destroyed by your enemies. You have no place in this assembly."

The President gestured for two burly mountain men to escort the now-weeping hydra from the forum. The look of longing Hydrane gave to Asher as she was dragged away made the halflings think that this was far from over.

The President came down the stairs from his dais and clasped his son firmly on the shoulders. "Oh Ash, it is so good to see you again. Please forgive an old man's mistake. In trying not to favour you, it appears I have believed the worst when there was no basis in truth. To think that I believed the word of a malicious hydra over my own flesh and blood. I now see that you have become a courageous man and have been acting to protect Relorians. You are indeed worthy to sit on this council."

With that, the President removed the heavy golden chains from his neck. "I will resign from the council from my lack of judgement in this matter." Asher looked stunned at his Father's declaration and as he turned his face, the mark of Hydrane's hand was clear on his cheek.

Aram placed his Presidential chains on the floor and turned to leave the forum. There was an outcry from the dais, quickly echoed by the watching masses around the forum.

One salt-and-pepper haired man from the council called out above the clamour, "No Aram, we do not want your resignation. In twenty years of wise ruling, this is the only time you have erred. Please come back and lead us. We have a war to plan against these Vergai and seek your wise counsel."

This statement was greeted with cheers from the crowd and cries of "Aram" and "Asher" rang out loudly amidst the uproar.

Aram Grey raised his hand for silence and spoke once more, "If it is the will of the people, I will continue to lead the council. Now let us deliberate and arrange a scouting party to check the western outpost. Come Ash and your friends, for there is a great deal we need to discuss." With that statement, the crowd began to exit the forum amid mutterings about both Hydrane's behaviour and the Vergai invasion.

As the room emptied, Mikel spoke in his friend's ear, "You'll need to watch your back against Hydrane now as well as Garass. You have made two deadly enemies there."

"I don't know what I could have done differently, my friend," Asher replied. "It amazes me that all this trouble was caused be my resisting her affections. After all, I was the innocent party. Hopefully once I come back from this quest, it will all be forgotten."

"Not likely with those two, but I hope so too," Mikel replied. "It looks to me as though Garass sees you as a threat to his chances of the Presidency."

The councillors relaxed on the dais, listening with surprise to Fendi's recount of their action-packed adventures. Sienna and the fairies interjected at times when he forgot small details, but Daeron spoke of the

Princess' capture. Aram was impressed to hear his errant son revealed as the leader of the hunters and a crucial force in the defence of Reloria.

There was an urgent need to get to the western outpost, though Aram Grey insisted they stay for dinner. Asher grumbled about the wasted time, but the companions were grateful for the short break and took the opportunity of a quick bathe in the thermal pools of Flame Mountain.

Asher's mother, Darna showed Sienna a private pool close to the family cave and the huntress enjoyed the soothing warm waters. Asher's youngest sister, Hennah gave Sienna some herbal oils for bathing and helped wash her long hair. She found the ladies to be very kind and gentle and not at all like the fierce savages the mountain folk were rumoured to be. While she bathed six women of the family prepared a delicious stew of goat and root vegetables, flavoured with many spices unfamiliar to the halflings.

Darna gave Sienna practical clothes to wear: warm furs for the cool winter's air and leather for their return journey. Touched, she thanked them for their kindness.

Sienna ate with the women in a cave decorated with colourful murals. There were three generations of the family there, with small children dancing and singing as their mothers worked. Sienna-Li was fascinated by the children and was welcomed by the playful youngsters, who gave him a tiny plate with a small meal of sweet fruits and a little bread.

The fairy had joined the children, who were playing with a tiny dragon, less than knee high, whom Darna introduced as Asher's one-year-old nephew, Fiream.

The young dragon's wings were not yet strong enough for him to fly properly so he did short bursts of furious wing-flapping, which barely got him off the ground, before he crashed into the fireplace. After bumping into a silvery dragon's egg, which was sitting amid the flames and coals, his mother, Hennah, smiling indulgently, admonished him and tossed him back among the children. Sienna-Li kept some distance away, for the little creature was trying to muster a flame, though he only managed smoke and a tiny spark. Yelping with frustration, he tried to fly again.

The women looked at him with adoration, however, and remarked how quickly he was growing and what a big, strong dragon he would be one day. Sienna asked if the egg was another baby shifter and Hennah proudly told her that, yes, her newest baby was due to hatch in a few weeks, barring accidental breakage from its clumsy brother Fiream. Sienna marvelled at these strange people, for while pampering her, the women spoke of the difficult teenage years of shifter life, when male dragons with an oversupply of testosterone sometimes fought to the death. They explained that Asher and Garass' disagreement stemmed back years ago to when they fought over a girl who was accidentally killed during their fight.

Darna and Hennah braided Sienna's hair in an elaborate style while another sister, Araya painted a henna dragon on the halfling's hand. The ladies all seemed genuinely delighted to pamper Sienna and invited her to return to visit them when her quest was over. The huntress was quite overwhelmed by all the female attention and happily agreed, comparing this life to that of growing up in the Wild Woods and hunting with only her father, or worse, her leering uncle.

CHAPTER 9: THE WESTERN OUTPOST

As soon as dinner was finished, the mountain women led Sienna outside to the men sitting by a campfire. Asher towered over the little halfling as he took her hand and gave her a bow, "Welcome huntress. You do look beautiful in your warrior clothes. We are honoured to fight alongside you." Fendi gave Sienna a wink, an admiring smile and handed her the longbow and quiver of arrows.

Just a few minutes later, six dragons were flying towards the western outpost in the Disputed Lands. The dragons were Ash, Mik, a black, a green, and red and maroon wyverns. Sienna clung tightly to Ash's scaly back as the large grey led them to rendezvous with the other hunters and their flying machine. Asher had put Daeron on the large black dragon and Fendi on Mik Dragon, so they could fly as fast as possible to the outpost.

It was a dark night, for the moon and the planet Zanarah were as yet hidden from view with only stars to light the night, but after several hours of flight, the planet appeared golden over the eastern horizon. Ash and Mik Dragon flew closely together so the halflings were able to call to each other across the distance.

"You awake, Fendi?" called Sienna, wiping sleep from her eyes after a long doze. She sighed, wishing she could snuggle in close against his warm body, for the early morning air was freezing cold and she pulled her warm fur cloak tighter around her.

"I'm worried about what we'll find at the Western Outpost," replied Fendi, eyes straining to make out dark shapes far to the west of them. As the dragons quickly closed the distance, the beasts let out screeches of alarm. Their keen eyes could discern clearly what were only vague blurs to the halflings.

"There's a large army ahead and it's not our alliance," declared Ash Dragon in a low growl.

"Should we turn back, Leader Ash?" asked a smaller green dragon named Klaw. "We are too few to attack so large an army."

"Don't worry, friend Klaw. Our task is to close the portal at the outpost and stop this part of the invasion.

These Vergai have not the means to attack us in the sky and we will be quite safe flying over them," Ash replied.

"What are those flashes of light near the western outpost?" asked the green dragon in alarm.

"Now that it a cause for concern," admitted Ash Dragon. "Chi'garu must have sent one of his Cyclopes here. They have a blazing light which burns from their single eye, so we must be wary of that one. Come, there's no time to waste. The hunters may be in danger."

The halflings clung on tightly while the dragons increased their speed with powerful wing thrusts.

Daeron called across to the other dragons from his large black dragon, "Remember not to engage the army on the ground. We need to take out the portal and return for reinforcements. Asher, are you listening to me?"

The big grey dragon gave the elf a steely look with his piercing yellowish eyes, "I will not be leaving this battlefield, until this filth on the ground breathes no more."

Fendi felt real fear at Ash's determined response, for there was no way that six dragons could defeat this large army. Mik Dragon turned to the smallest of the wyverns, "Return to the council and tell them of the armies amassed here," he said. "They need to send every dragon they can muster, even the hydras. Messengers must be sent to all our allies to hasten to our aid. These invaders must be defeated before their ships arrive, or our forces will be spread too thin and we will be crushed."

The maroon wyvern nodded his head and banking sharply, set off toward Flame Mountain.

Ash Dragon sped towards the invading army massing ahead of them. Now the halflings could make out what the elf and dragons had already seen; the grasslands ahead were covered with thousands of Vergai, spread out in numerous camps across the land, and beyond them, the outpost castle was just discernible in the early morning gloom. Bolts of lightning could be seen striking about the black fortress. As they sped closer, Fendi saw many giants surrounding the crackling portal.

Uncertainty about the dark shadows above the portal caused Ash Dragon to slow his rapid pace and the five dragons hovered high above the Vergai campfires.

"There be some kind of sorcery here!" Ash growled. "See those large blobs suspended over the castle? They emit lightning at random intervals. To destroy the portal we must avoid them if we are to defeat the wizards on the other side."

To the dragons' surprise, a loud voice came from far above them, "Well, it's about time you dragons joined the party. We have been here for hours, but can't find a way past the lightning creatures and the giants. They keep pouring through the portal and we can't get close to it." It was Baja's voice calling, but he sounded rather more serious than usual.

They looked up to see Heikki's gnomish flying machine suspended above them, with their companions straining to look over the sides of the basket.

Fendi gave a big grin and wave at the sight of his friends, "Randir, Baja, Raja, Sir Varnon, Vi and Heikki. You did beat us here. What are we going to do?"

Sir Varnon spoke, "Well met, fellow hunters. I was hoping you would devise a plan. We cannot get close enough for Violetta to perform her magic, so I suggest we distract the giants, allowing you dragons to breathe your fire through the portal. You will have to dodge those lightning..." The rest of his sentence has lost in the surprise as a huge dark form swooped out of the sky and crashed into Ash Dragon.

"Traitor!" yelled a raspy voice.

The hunters cried out in alarm as the mighty Garass Dragon sent scorching flames towards the hot air balloon. Violetta was heard chanting and the balloon rose rapidly away from the entangled dragons. Fendi called out in panic from the back of Mik Dragon, as Ash was spun upside down and Sienna clung on to the rope harness around his neck for dear life. Her arrows spilled from her quiver and rained down upon the Vergai far below.

Mik called out to the black attacker, "Garass, you fool. Can't you see that we are about to attack a huge host of invaders? Surely you must realise that Ash only did what was best for the Mountain Men."

Garass Dragon paused for a minute; taking in the sight of thousands of Vergai camped below them with giants and lightning creatures surrounding the castle. He pulled away from the grey, studying the invading force.

Ash Dragon had righted himself and Fendi was relieved to see Sienna still clinging tightly around the dragon's spiked neck. Ash spoke in a husky voice, "Our disagreement must wait Garass. More invaders are coming every minute and we must close that portal. Come and help me distract the giants."

206

Garass gave a small nod and a cry was heard from above them.

"Noooo," shouted the voice of Hydrane, the enormous hydra as large as the grey and black dragons. Her dark blue dragon body was topped by two long, graceful necks with fierce heads. "No, you must fight for me. Garass, Asher, who loves me the most? Prove your love by slaying the other." She had managed to turn her two mighty heads so that one locked glances with each of them.

Garass Dragon gave a deep, throaty roar and swatted her with his long, barbed tail, "You mad hydra! Neither of us wants you now, so come and fight, or go home to your watery nest. We must defend the western lands for Flame Mountain." With that, the large black dragon rose into the air and shouted, "Come Ash, we'll fight as brothers."

The persistent hydra determinedly followed Garass, while the others ignored her.

Ash Dragon took one last look at the Hunters of Reloria in the flying machine, "Lead them to the wizards, Varnon. If I fail, that is our last hope."

With mighty beats of his wings, the dragon set off towards the portal, leaving his companions behind. Fendi gave a cry of despair at seeing Sienna valiantly clinging to his spiked neck. Garass followed him closely, the others with Daeron riding on Coal Black.

As they approached the castle, Fendi saw it was the same defensive design as the other outposts, but made of black rock. A fair distance in front of the castle was the portal, surrounded by giants and twelve of the strange lightning creatures. Fendi thought that they looked a bit like large bloated toads, anchored to the ground in front of the portal by long thick ropes. Glowing, antennae projecting from their foreheads were suspended before wide mouths. Every so often, one of the creatures burped and lightning crackled in all directions, striking the ground with a loud explosion and the giants stayed well clear of them, positioned directly in front of the portal.

Ash Dragon reached the space above the portal first and circling high above it, he saw the portal could only be seen from the eastern side, with no guards to the west and surmised that the portal could only be accessed from one direction. The other dragons, hydra and wyvern, waited for his lead.

"Follow me, dragons, we'll go straight down the middle and then peel off sideways just before the portal, sending our strongest burst of flame into the portal's mouth. Let's go."

His wings beating strongly, Ash Dragon sped straight towards the lightning creatures, with the others fanning out behind in a V formation. As they flew lower over the army encampments, Fendi realised that there were only a handful of Vergai below them and that most of the sleeping army were two-eyed giants.

This was a race of people the hunters had not encountered before. Their skin was more orange than the Cyclops' honey skin and they wore leather straps crossing their broad chests, their heads shaved bald. There were no visible weapons around the campfires, so Fendi wondered what their fighting style could be.

As the dragons descended, they were detected by the guards below who raised the alarm. Fendi spied a giant turning the handle on a box which emitted the metallic whirring noise and watched with dismay as all of the enemy fighters roused from their sleep and arranged in battle formation. Luckily the dragons flew so fast that by the time most of the invaders were ready to fight, they were far away.

Approaching the portal, shouts were heard from the one-eyed giants below, "Cyclopes, gather around the portal." "Make sure the Junda soldiers are ready in case the dragons come to the ground. Pounce on them to prevent them flying away." "Tether the Ildirim at different heights to ensure the dragons can't get through."

Fendi saw the Ildirims' ropes being adjusted, as the Junda soldiers tried to avoid the lightning bolts landing sporadically around them. One of the giant soldiers was struck by a bolt and killed instantly. The others rolled him aside and continued adjusting the ropes as if nothing had happened.

The dragons approached the Ildirim rapidly with Ash Dragon urging them back in a single file. He started to wend his way through the floating creatures. Bolts of lightning crackled around him and static electricity filled the air. Sienna closed her eyes and hung on tightly as Ash swerved to avoid the blasts. One bolt crashed so close that it made her squeal with fright and cling closer to the big grey.

The other dragons bravely followed him, ducking though the random bolts of lightning and the crackling energy made Fendi's hair stand on end as he clung tightly to Mik Dragon.

210

After ducking under one low lightning creature, Fendi heard a bolt strike close behind him. He turned his neck sharply to see that the green dragon Klaw had been struck and was falling lifelessly to the ground. Fendi-La gave a cry of alarm and buried her tiny head in Fendi's chest, and he was lost for words to console the tiny fairy. Fear knotted his stomach and he whispered a prayer for luck to keep them safe.

After what seemed an eternity, they reached the end of the deadly Ildirim and were faced with the Cyclopes guarding the portal. Their large eyes glowed red as the dragons approached and they burst into blinding beams of white-hot light. The dragons ducked and weaved in random evasions to avoid the deadly rays. Asher slowed to check his progress and the other dragons caught up to him.

The little red wyvern took the initiative, darting close to the nearest Cyclops. He turned as he closed with the giant, piercing him in the neck with his poisonous tail barb. The Cyclops gave a gasp of pain and the light beam disappeared. He grabbed at his neck and gave a choking cough before dropping to the ground. Fendi gave a small cheer, "Go Raish!"

Raish was very speedy and managed to dart in and spear another giant with his poison, before a deadly beam of light brushed his wing tip. He screeched in pain and retreated as Garass and Ash bravely flew past belching fire across the line of Cyclopes, followed by Mik and Coal.

Hydrane and Raish brought up the rear and looking backwards, Daeron watched on in horror, as the small red wyvern was severed in two by a sudden change in direction of the Cyclops's deadly beam. The severed body of the wyvern fell to the ground and twitched for a few seconds before becoming still. Daeron took a deep breath, gritted his teeth and tightened his hold on the big black dragon.

Hydrane screeched and spewed her poisonous breath across another Cyclops, instantly killing the giant creature. One of her long necks was severed by a beam of light and Fendi saw two buds appear, quickly growing into two more necks and heads. It made her appear even more fearsome as she threw her three heads back in a piercing screech. Her bright blue scales gleamed in the lightning and hairy tuffs standing up on her large heads made her look even more fearsome. Her silver eyes glowed with malevolence and Sienna gave silent thanks that she was finally on their side.

The battle continued, with dragons flying in random passes through the lines of Cyclopes, and the hydra using her poison. Despite coming at different angles on each pass, they were unable to reach the portal for the light beams crisscrossed the sky in unpredictable patterns. Occasionally the beams touched each other and sparks erupted, causing the Cyclops to wince and draw away from each other.

After one such incident, sparks showered through the air and both Cyclopes took a step backwards. Coal, the big black dragon took advantage of their lapse in attention and tried to dart his huge body through the gap. One of the Cyclopes raised his beam, searing across the dragon's left wing and chest and Coal gave an agonised screech of pain. Daeron tried to jump clear of him, but the Cyclopes were too close, so he hung on tightly instead. Rather than crash straight to the ground, the big black dragon aimed directly for the portal, and with a desperate beat of his remaining wing, disappeared through the black gateway.

The other dragons cried out in alarm, except Ash Dragon who quickly ducked between two deadly beams and followed the big black through. Sienna and her fairy bowed their heads low as the grey dragon skimmed the top of the portal, which shimmered for an instant and was gone. Fendi cried out in vain, but the portal was no more, so they flew through the place it had been and over the western outpost to safety.

Garass, Hydrane and Mik were all that were left of the strike force. Fendi covered his face with his hands and cried out in anguish at the loss of Asher, Daeron and his Sienna. "No, no, they can't be gone. We had almost done it. Another few minutes and we would have sent fire through the portal and closed it."

"Steady youngster," soothed Mik Dragon's hoarse voice. "Ash is not one to throw his life away. I believe that he went through that portal for a reason, even if it's not clear to us. He must have a plan to fight the enemy from wherever he is now. Don't despair, for he is the strongest and bravest of us all."

Fendi felt something bump the back of his head and looked up to find the flying machine above him with a rope ladder hanging down. "Keep still for a minute there Mik," he said grabbing hold of the rope, and he climbed up to the shocked hunters waiting above, who greeted him with hugs, and quiet tears from Violetta. "Well, what do we do now?" he asked sadly. Randir and Baja held him up, for his legs started to wobble with shock.

"We do as Ash would have wanted, young halfling," said Sir Varnon stoically, trying hard to maintain his composure. "We continue our quest towards the wizard's stronghold and seek their aid to create our own portal."

He turned to the wizard's apprentice, who was sitting up on the side of the basket, her hair fashioned in a tall cone on her head and large butterfly wings gently flapping at her back. "Now girl, you must tell us how to get to the Wizard's stronghold. And no more stalling."

"Of course," Violetta replied. "We'll have to head up to the Diagro Plains and borrow some snow dogs to head further north to the Ice Lands. I'd be happy to give you more details as we go along and…"

"A straight answer," exclaimed Baja in surprise. "Well that's something I never thought I'd hear from you, witch."

"Witch!" screeched Violetta. "I'll have you know that I am a well-trained apprentice and have abilities in all of the elements. Why if I so desired, I'd turned you into a pig and your brother would have to carry you around, so you didn't get eaten. I don't take kindly to…."

Raja stopped her there. "Not now, our talented apprentice, for we need your skills and guidance to get us to the wizards' stronghold. All members of the Hunters of Reloria are important and we need Baja to remain a dwarf, so don't do anything rash. Now let's farewell these dragons and be on our way."

Violetta calmed down and Heikki arranged the balloon to hover near the dragons so the knight could speak with them. "Our thanks to you brave dragons for your assistance in closing the portal, but we are truly saddened by the losses of Klaw, Raish and Coal. Hopefully Ash Dragon is well and we will meet him again. As you can see, this war is building rapidly and we implore you to seek the aid of the other dragons of Flame Mountain. The maroon wyvern is even now informing the mountain council of the magnitude of this invasion with elves, dwarves, goblins and centaurs coming from the Elven Heart. We hunters will go to seek the aid of the knights, for we must rescue the elven princess from the enemy's hands. Remember, speed is vital, so we must be on our way. Farewell and thanks."

"Goodbye and good luck," echoed the answering cries as the dragons headed south and the flying machine banked towards the north.

Baja hefted some of the gnomish explosives over the side of the balloon basket and chuckled as loud bangs exploded in the giants' encampment below them. "I wish I'd managed to blow up some of those Cyclopes," he said.

Pushing the red buttons on the last two incendiaries he threw them casually over his shoulder as the flying machine left the camp behind, leaving the giants milling around like a nest of angry ants.

"Look how red that sunrise is this morning," remarked Raja, as the sun rose spectacularly in the east. Heikki and the remaining hunters dejectedly gazed at the sky and wondered about their future while Violetta conjured up her wind spell.

Randir grimly quoted a proverb, "Red skies at morning, halfling take warning," then added, "There's more bloodshed to come, you can be sure of that."

CHAPTER 10: ZANARAH

On a strange orange planet, Coal crashed through several wizards and their Vergai guards and came to rest at the foot of a squadron of Junda soldiers. The black dragon shuddered as his last breath escaped him.

One of the giants picked up Daeron and threw him hard to the ground. Dazed and lightheaded by the blow, he struggled to draw his sword. The Junda picked him up as though he was a feather and flipped him onto his back, made a chopping motion to Daeron's head and the elf sank into unconsciousness.

A split second later, Ash Dragon and Sienna hurtled through the gateway knocking over the remaining wizards and the portal disappeared in a crackle of static energy.

"Seize them," yelled a female Cyclops, who wore a tight black cloth bustier, black kilt and carried a long whip wound around her golden shoulders. She was exceptionally tall, even for a Cyclops, and uncoiling the glowing whip, she lashed the spot where Ash Dragon had just leapt upwards from the ground. The giants ducked to avoid his long barbed tail and he escaped rapidly into the strange orange sky.

Shaking his head to try and settle the feelings of dizziness and nausea, Ash Dragon noticed something different about this place. A single beat of his wings took him twice as high as it would back in Reloria but the air seemed somehow thinner, making it more difficult to breathe. Ascending rapidly, Ash circled the former portal site.

Looking down he saw Coal's human body lying on the ground with the huge gash across his chest and blood was spilling onto the ground. With several dead wizards and Vergai scattered in the brown mud, Ash assumed that the portal would remain closed for some time.

Daeron looked unconscious, trapped under a Junda guard's large foot and Ash could see no way to rescue the fallen elf, surrounded by two Cyclopes, around two hundred Junda and several chained wizards with their Vergai guards. He saw the Junda pick Daeron up as though he weighed nothing, but the bodies of the dead remained lying in the mud.

Sienna and her fairy held tightly to the grey dragon, the huntress' eyes absorbing their new surroundings. This place was clearly very different to Reloria. Not only were the inhabitants enormous and intimidating, the land was a brown marsh almost as far as the eye could see. The only visible building was an imposing-looking fortress, which seemed to grow out of the brown swampy ground, and to which the enemy were taking Daeron.

Continuing her reconnaissance of the area, she saw these were the only people visible in the area. Muddy streams crisscrossed the landscape, and there were a few large pockets of trees amongst the brown marsh, though these were the exception, rather than the rule.

Sienna felt Ash Dragon's wings momentarily falter and she called out to him, "Are you alright Ash? You must be close to exhaustion."

The great grey turned his head to the side and said, "I must rest for a while Huntress. I pray that Daeron is alive and would try to rescue him, but I fear we'd also be overwhelmed. Let us fly away from here and find somewhere to recharge my energy. Are you able to stand guard, for I fear for our safety in this land?"

"Of course Ash," she replied confidently. "I'll make sure you are not disturbed, but what a strange fate for us to end up here on Zanarah. I wonder if the Princess is in that immense fortress. Could that be the Ar'gon Tower? If so it will be well-guarded. Do you have a plan?"

"Not yet, young one," he replied, "But we will think of something. We are survivors, you and I. An answer will present itself." Sometime later Ash Dragon set down in a patch of woodland before shape-shifting. After surveying the immediate area, Sienna realised it was unlike any forest she had ever seen. The air was warm and humid and the solid tree trunks were covered in fungus and lichen. She slowly started sinking in the mud, and Asher extended a human hand to help her onto a tree branch. He climbed up several more until he found a space where he could safely prop himself up to sleep. Sienna helped to rope him securely to the branches and within a minute he was falling asleep, so she left her fur cloak and climbed down the tree again.

"Well, little fairy," she said to Sienna-Li, "What do you think those giants eat? Let's have a little look around this strange place. I feel so light here; almost as though I could fly." Jumping upwards, she hit her head on a tree branch high above her head. "Ouch."

She fell to the ground and sank up to her waist in mud. Sienna-Li hovered just out of reach chuckling. "What are you laughing at, cheeky boy?"

Sienna-Li nodded his tiny head until his bell tinkled. "I was just thinking how much fun the Princess would be having if she was here, waist deep in mud. She'd be screeching her pretty elven head off. I would so love to see that." He grinned impishly and fluttered his iridescent wings. "I feel light as a feather here."

Sienna had her carving knife out and was whittling a point on a long stick. "I lost all my arrows in that battle back in Reloria," she told the fairy. I'll make some more later on, but for now I'll make do with a spear, so keep an eye out for potential dinner." When the spear was sharpened, she went looking for food in the muddy forest.

Water was flowing across the ground, making it even boggier than before, forcing her to jump from tree to tree.

A short distance away from the sleeping Asher, she saw a bald cat-like creature quietly slinking along a low branch over the rapidly rising water. The creature pounced; catching a fish from the shallow water and with a very sharp set of teeth began to eat. Sienna threw the spear and the cat-creature tumbled into the quickly moving water and Sienna scooped it up before it floated away. The spear had penetrated the fish as well, so she took both back to Asher and tied them to the end of his rope. She went hunting a number of times over the next two hours, and was rewarded with another of the cat-like creatures, a scaly reptile and several more fish.

Sienna and her fairy then rested on a branch near Asher. The water level seemed to have settled at about a foot deep, coinciding with both the moon and blue planet appearing above them in the sky. As evening came, they disappeared below the horizon and the water left as quickly as it had come.

"Do you think that is really Zumar up there?" Sienna-Li asked quietly. He was playing with flowers he had collected and had one yellow flower upside-down on his head like a hat while drinking the nectar from another.

"I guess it must be," Sienna replied with a sigh. "It's the strangest thing to know that you are a world away from home and have no idea if you'll ever return. I'm going to miss Fendi the most and all the adventures we had together. He must be wondering what's happened to us."

Sienna sighed wistfully and the fairy wisely changed the subject, "When's this big oaf going to wake up and cook dinner for you? You must be starving after not eating for the whole day."

A smelly sock swung through the air and caught the fairy by surprise, sending him spinning towards the mud before his wings lifted him up.

"Cheeky fairy," Asher muttered, "Am I to be stuck in this desolate place with you for company?" He scratched his hair and remarked on the biting insects which were coming with the approaching darkness. He shimmered, returning him to dragon form, springing into the air when the branch broke and fell to the marshy ground below.

Rising quickly, he hovered just above the canopy, where with a small burst of flame, he seared the meat and fish until it was cooked.

The hungry Sienna gratefully tucked into her meal, then curled up under her cloak to avoid the biting midges, her bow, knife and newly-made arrows within easy reach. Singing quietly, Sienna-Li grew his mushroom bed on a nearby branch while Sienna slept and Ash Dragon flew off into the moonless night. Soon the only sounds were the unfamiliar cries of nocturnal animals hunting for food.

*   *   *

Back on the planet Zumar, Randir gave a sigh of relief that Violetta had finally stopped talking and was curled up in the bottom of the balloon basket next to Raja. "I hope she sleeps for the whole day," he whispered to Fendi. I understand that we need her skills and knowledge, but she's very tiresome to live with. At least Asher was able to quieten her down a bit."

Fendi nodded, "I wish Ash and Sienna were here too. We're not the Hunters of Reloria without them. We've really only known them for a short time, but I can hardly imagine my life now without them. Asher is our leader and mentor on this strange journey and Sienna is….." he broke off, suddenly lost for words.

"I know," Randir filled in the silence. "Sienna is very special to you, isn't she? When you both lost your fathers, you found solace with each other. She is the first halfling you have been in love with and your life will not be complete without her. I can only imagine what being so deeply in love must be like. Keep believing that we will find a way to reach her, Fendi."

Fendi nodded sadly, surprised at how well his friend read his feelings. Randir may be clumsy and rarely serious, but he was a true friend. Fendi looked up at Randir's stubbled chin and knew that even though they had travelled far from Southdale, they were even further away from the boys they had once been. They were now halfling men and had been in battles that their friends could never have imagined. They would never again be the same carefree children running through grain fields and teasing the village girls. None of whom were a patch on his fierce huntress, who now seemed lost forever. Randir patted him gently on the shoulder as he bowed his head.

There had been a look of fierceness about her beautiful dark eyes and a courage born of fending for herself in the Wild Woods. Fendi had admired the way she would take on the Vergai without fear or hesitation. She had embarked on this quest with them, not knowing where it would lead or what dangers would befall them, and Fendi realised that had it not been for her courage, they all might have turned back when they had discovered the Princess had been kidnapped. Fendi was now even more determined to continue their mission and save not just the Elven Jewel, but his huntress as well.

"Fear not, young halflings," Sir Varnon said, "Your friend is in the hands of one of Reloria's finest. I would trust that mountain man with my life...and you know what a strong statement that is, coming from a Diagro knight. Now, have you seen the townships below? We are flying over the Diagro Plains and the kingdom of my father."

The halflings peered over the high rim of the basket to see the grass plains and farming towns below, and Randir felt a twinge of homesickness at the crop fields and cottages with smoking chimneys. Instead of the thatched roofs of the South Lands, these sturdy houses had steep wooden sloping roofs to prevent snow build-up. The towns and farms were surrounded by high walls with spikes on the tops and some had catapults lying idle. One township they passed over had been completely gutted by fire. "Dragons," growled Sir Varnon, a fierce look in his eye at the visual reminder of the centuries of hostility between the races.

 The winter's chill increased the further north they flew, and now the trees' branches were bare. The halflings shared a thin blanket they had found in the bottom of the basket, while Randir's stomach growled loudly when he thought of how little food they'd had since leaving the elves.

"I hope the knights will have a good feed for us," said Baja hopefully. "I've seen some plump-looking animals on the farms we've been flying over. Does your father keep deer, Varnon?"

"King Varl has the finest game in all of Reloria and I am sure that he will welcome us warmly," replied the knight. "It will be good to see home again, even if only briefly, for we must leave early tomorrow."

With the aid of Violetta's magical powers, the flying machine arrived at Varx Castle just as the sun set that same day. The surrounding farmlands were ploughed in neat squares like a chequerboard, with an extensive forest extending to the north. An impressively large castle occupied an entire hill above a city of stone buildings that sprawled across the surrounding plains. The citadel was surrounded by three separate defensive walls and beyond them, a wide moat with four crossings, each with a raised drawbridge, jutting out into the moat like the points on a gnomish compass.

With many tall towers of varying heights, this was the largest castle in all of Reloria. The defensive walls were as thick as a house to make them immune to dragon fire. Sharp-tipped spears were built into the battlements. Randir and Fendi were speechless at the magnitude of it all, the catapults loaded and ready with powerful ballistae mounted on the tall towers.

Unlike the halflings, Violetta seemed unimpressed, babbling incessantly of other things as they set the balloon down in the large courtyard inside the castle walls. Heikki bade the companions goodbye then, for he was worried that the cool air might ground his balloon. They were sorry to farewell the friendly and colourful old gnome, who took off again into the early evening air, just as light snow began to fall.

"Brrrr," shivered Fendi, "Let's get inside quickly."

The hunters had just turned to approach the castle, when something large and sticky fell on them from above. It was a huge rope net covered in sticky black tar, so heavy that it knocked them to the cobblestones. Sir Varnon landed hard on his head and lost consciousness.

"Vergai are coming to take over the castle!" yelled Violetta in her loudest voice.

Raja clapped a hairy hand over her mouth and hissed, "Shush" in her ear. The wizard's apprentice heeded the warning for once and remained silent, but it was too late.

Voices could be heard from atop the battlements. "You see, they admit they are the invading Vergai. Guards, prepare to burn the invaders." Iron-reinforced wooden doors swung open and twenty knights dressed in heavy armour surrounded them, pointing long wooden pikes at the hunters. Another knight followed with a flaming torch.

Baja and Raja tried to stand and draw their axes, but the heavy net made that impossible, and the more they wriggled, the more they became covered in the sticky black tar.

Randir cried out in panic, as the knight with the flame grew nearer, "Wait! There's been a mistake. We are Relorians, come to seek the aid of King Varl. Please listen to us."

The knights paused, but the voice on the wall cried out, "Do not listen to these strangers who have invaded our citadel. They would open our gates to their hordes of merciless fighters and destroy all we hold dear. Only today we received a rider from the Elven Heart who warned us that an invasion by the Vergai is imminent. Burn them all and do it quickly!"

230

The knights took a step backward, as the burning torch approached, but the hunters heard Violetta muttering a spell under her breath and a cold wind blew, extinguishing the torch, and as it blew harder, the knights in armour froze into white statues.

"I guess I shouldn't complain that it's a bit cold," said Baja in an attempt at humour. His teeth were chattering from both the cold and narrowly avoiding being burned alive. "That was pretty scary, for a minute. Thank-you Violetta," he said as they extracted themselves from the sticky net.

"We owe you a great debt," said Sir Varnon groggily, nursing his sore head. "Now, we must unravel this confusion before they bring out the burning pitch." He rose to his feet and, leaning heavily on the two dwarves, called to the knight in the battlements, "Well met, friend knights. But it is I, Sir Varnon, come to see my father the King."

"Sir Varnon, can it be true?" answered a familiar voice. There was the clatter of boots rushing down stone stairs and the castle gates opened, revealing Sir Jerephey and Varnon's squire Jacab running toward them. Young Jacab almost bowled his lord over as he gave him a bear hug. "Are you a'right my Lord? You seem rather unsteady on your feet. Oh to think that you were almost burned as invaders. It is too horrible to contemplate!"

"Steady now, young Jacab, try not to knock your Prince over," chastised Sir Jerephey good-naturedly. "It is good to see you again, Varnon, and we do humbly apologise for the confusion. That flying contraption looked like a foreign invasion to these knights. By the way, could you please unfreeze them?"

Everyone turned to Violetta who looked rather sheepishly at the frozen knights surrounding them. "Will they be nice to me now? I didn't really like the welcome they gave us and maybe it would be easier to leave..."

"Violetta!" the hunters cried in unison.

"Release them, or you will sleep here in the snow," boomed a voice from the castle gate.

The hunters looked up to see an elderly knight wearing thick furs strolling through the gates. His curly hair was grey and there were scars across one cheek, but the hunters saw clearly the resemblance and realised that this was Varnon's father. Sir Varnon, Sir Jerephey and Jacab bowed low when greeting their King.

Varl, King of the Diagro Plains gave his son a warm welcome and politely greeted the unexpected visitors. "I heard you were travelling with an elf and a mountain man as well. Are they here?"

"They are lost, my Lord," said Fendi sadly. "And a halfling was lost with them. We don't know their fate, but we hasten north to seek help from the wizards."

The King looking down intently at the earnest young halfling, "I am sorry for your loss, young halfling. You remind me of a halfling I knew as a boy. I expect you might know him. His name was Fandri from the Southdale and he had the most beautiful fairy I ever saw."

"He was my Father, your highness," Fendi replied proudly. "He died fighting the Vergai in the Zanzi Grasslands. Many times he spoke fondly of you and your life here in the north."

Sir Varnon introduced the companions to his father while Violetta released the frozen knights. The apprentice even obliged by warming the air to dry the dripping knights, who looked rather perplexed at finding out who the presumed Vergai invaders really were.

King Varl jovially welcomed his guests while patting his rather ample girth, hidden beneath a red fur-lined cloak. He called for a feast of venison and pork to feed the hungry travellers, Randir and Baja followed behind him, wide smiles on their faces.

*   *   *

King Varl and Queen Gwendolyn's long dining table groaned under the weight of the feast. Varnon sat at his father's right and Fendi to the Queen's left, telling of their adventures since leaving the South Lands. The King listened closely, asking questions about the treaty, and what they might expect from the invasion. He told them that on receiving the news that afternoon, he had sent riders to alert the forts along the coastline. The messenger had also told of the mermaids coming to help fight the invading ships, though the King was clearly disinclined to ally himself with these 'scourges of the sea' as he described them.

Sitting in her dining chair, Violetta amused herself by playing a harp across the room using air magic. She and the bond-fairies chuckled at the consternation of the minstrels. At least her concentration on the music slowed down her usually incessant talking, Randir decided.

Halfway through dinner there was a noisy entrance of a tall blonde lady with a new baby in her arms, a toddler clinging to her skirt and two other young children, all racing across the dining hall. She embraced Sir Varnon and showered him with hugs and kisses, to the cheers of the knights. After many minutes of warm greetings, the prince introduced his wife, Lady Elsabet and their children Barond, Rolund, Eloise, and the one who brought a tear to her father's eyes, the new baby as yet unnamed.

"I am so relieved you have returned to us, dear husband," said the beautiful Elsabet, with tears in her eyes. "Has the King told you that you are the last of your six brothers? Young Warram was killed by the dragons not three weeks ago on our side of the disputed lands. I am so very sorry for your loss Varnon."

Sir Varnon looked with shock from his father to his mother. "Warram too? All of my five brothers killed by the dragons. It is hard to comprehend."

"They will pay for this," roared King Varl, disturbing the silence that had settled upon the family reunion. His wrinkled face turned an angry purple and veins stood out on his neck. "We will not rest until every last dragon and mountain man has been killed to avenge their deaths. I will honour no treaty with these renegades. They are more likely to stab us in the back than fight alongside us."

Fendi cautiously stepped forward and knelt before the King, "My Lord, I have been to the council of Flame Mountain and heard the Mountain President declare that the war with the knights is over and we are allies against the Vergai. We have all learnt from the first Vergai war that it is impossible to defeat them without the strength of the mountain men."

King Varl was bright red with emotion and took several deep breaths to calm the instinctive insults desperate to roll from his tongue. "Fendi, son of my friend Fandri, I have no quarrel with you. I caution you to forget this treaty and pursue this with me no further. The mountain men have not earned our loyalty and I am in no mood to listen to your attempts to sway me. We will defend the Diagro Plains and they can rot on their mountain!"

Fendi was at a loss as how to proceed with his attempts at persuasion and wisely changed the subject by complimenting the Queen on the fine food being served at their long dining table. He would bide his time and try to broach the subject when the King was more relaxed.

* * *

The feast ended and it was now time to celebrate and name the new baby. The halflings were baffled by the strange practice of pouring ale over the screaming baby, then catching the drips and drinking them to toast the baby's health. Baja at least approved of this custom and participated in the drinking with gusto.

"We name her Gwendolyn, Princess of the Diagro Plains; named after her beautiful grandmother, the Queen," declared Sir Varnon to the raucous assembly. Lifting the screaming baby he passed her to his mother who happily received her and wrapped her in clean linens. Fendi watched the obvious love within the family as grandmother and baby cuddled together and he pondered that perhaps their hearts were not so different from those of the mountain men they despised.

Lady Elsabet gave her husband another hug. "We have missed you at Rowland Manor, Varnon. Will you be home soon?"

This made the big knight frown, "Alas my love, there is still the quest foretold by the Ancient Oracle. I cannot say where it will take me or even if I will be home again. I must urge you take the children to the safety of the Elven Heart. There may be rough times ahead for the plainsmen, but I promise to return as soon as I possibly can, so please do not worry, for I have many fine companions with me."

He gestured towards the minstrels, where Raja played his pan pipes and Baja, Randir, Fendi and their fairies were merrily dancing with young Diagro maidens. Baja even managed to dance with two pretty girls simultaneously, while gulping a tankard of foaming ale. Violetta had transformed into a violet-eyed cat, playing hide-and-seek with the children while being chased by Varnon's large bloodhound, Rusty.

"Hmm…" mused the knight. "I guess they are just unwinding after our adventures. I hope they will be ready to leave at dawn tomorrow!" This last comment was directed toward the three partying companions on the dance floor, who waved as they turned their attention to a buxom lass holding three full tankards of ale.

*   *   *

The snow continued falling throughout the night, blanketing the castle. Peering through the glass window Randir groaned, "Are you awake Fendi? The sun is well up already but there's snow covering the ground. We are going to freeze!"

Fendi rolled over and murmured, "Just a little longer. I'm asleep. I was having the nicest dream about Sienna kissing me and…."   His brown face turned a bright crimson at the thought of what Sienna's embrace had been doing to his hormone-charged teenage body.

"I bet Fendi-La will tell me all about your dream," teased Randir-La and grabbed Fendi's bond fairy by the arm.

Fendi-La shook her head and her bell rang, saying, "You know the fairy code Randir-La and I will not be the one to break it. Fendi's romantic dreams are safe with me." The sweet fairy looked a little shy at having shared her halfling's dream. "You know, I can't wait to see Sienna-Li again. He is too cute!"

Fendi groaned, missing Sienna even more. He rolled over in bed. "I'll just have a quick nap until it's time to leave," he muttered.

"No time for that," replied Sir Varnon from the doorway. "You have five minutes for breakfast, or you'll be travelling on an empty stomach." He pulled the blankets off Fendi and threw them on the floor. "I do have some good news for you halflings," he added. "I managed to obtain warm furs for you to wear. It will get colder the farther north we go." He dropped a pile of small fur clothes on the floor.

The good news was not well received. "Colder!" yelped the halflings in unison, hurriedly dressing in the new furs. Snow never fell in the South Lands and the thought of it getting colder than this was frightening to the youngsters.

In the dining hall, they stopped in surprise to see Baja spoon feeding porridge to two of the young lasses he had been dancing with last night. He was whispering in their ears while they giggled cheekily. "We wish you didn't have to leave Baja Stormhammer," lamented one girl. "You have taught us so much about dwarves already and we'll miss you."

"Ah wee lassie," drawled Baja "We'll be back again before you know it." He winked knowingly at Randir and gave an almost imperceptible nod to a well-dressed young lady eating by herself at the end of the long breakfast table. The halfling gave a 'not-my-business' shrug of his shoulders, concentrating instead on the intoxicating aromas coming from covered dishes on the long table.

Raja was just finishing his breakfast of eggs and bacon when the halflings sat down, but then they heard barking down in the courtyard and it was time to go. Grabbing what food they could they hurried after the dwarf.

In the castle courtyard a crowd had gathered around a large pack of woolly dogs and six sleds piled high with provisions. The dogs were being harnessed together in groups of eight by Sir Jerephey who had volunteered to care for the animals and help them navigate the snow lands. Fendi noticed that one of the dogs was unleashed. Closer inspection revealed it to be a pure white wolf with violet eyes. Fendi chuckled and patted her. "Good form mage," he whispered.

Violetta had given Sir Jerephey directions for the first leg of their journey north. The snow was too shallow for the hunters to ride the sleds at first so they walked alongside them down the steep ramp, through the city streets and on into the dense northern forest. Sir Varnon's family followed them to the edge of the city, showering the knight with hugs before they departed.

Embracing him fiercely, Lady Elsabet loudly whispered that his duty was to come back to his family and watch his children grow big and strong. He was the last of six strong brothers, and his father would be devastated to lose him, not to mention his young family. The others pretended not to notice the misty-eyed emotion on the face of the battle-hardened knight. Giving his wife a passionate kiss, he briefly cradled his baby daughter in his arms before hurrying along the snowy trail after the other hunters. His two boys Barond and Rolund accompanied them a short distance but were called back, still waving when their father was hidden by the falling snow.

CHAPTER 11: THE AR'GON TOWER

The Elven Jewel of Reloria, Princess Shari-Rose, was tethered to a long stout rope held by Master Ab'hijit, the cruel Cyclops who had been left in charge of Zanarah in the Emperor's absence. Most of the Ar'gon Tower's forces had left to invade Reloria, some by portal to the Western Outpost and many others accompanied Emperor Chi'garu to Vergash where the battleships awaited them.

No sooner had Chi'garu gone through the portal, than Ab'hijit forced the Princess to grovel at his feet like a slave and it was only the Emperor's command that she remain untouched that had kept her from further humiliations. The new leader frequently made leering comments and offensive gestures which made the young elf cringe as far from him as her leash would allow.

Shari-Rose worried about her guardian Daeron, now locked in a dank cell without windows or furniture. Ab'hijit had overturned the Emperor's rule of keeping

243

Daeron comfortable, torturing and starving him until he was too weak to attempt escape. Twice Ab'hijit had taken her to see Daeron in an attempt to frighten her into compliance. The Princess tried hard to remain defiant and prayed that somehow they were rescued before he succumbed to the ill-treatment.

The Princess had been trying her magic on her captor only to discover to her horror that these giants were immune to magic. Elven magic was basically defensive in nature, unlike the offensive elemental powers of the wizards of Nnanell and apart from the listening spell, her magic was ineffective to the point that Shari-Rose doubted she would be able to escape while under constant guard.

There was one faint cause for hope, however. It appeared that as well as the black dragon who died crashing through and killing many wizards, there had also been a grey dragon, which had eluded capture. Master Ab'hijit had been enraged and immediately killed the Junda messenger who brought this news. He ordered Daeron be tortured for information on what threat this dragon posed for the Zanarahns, though the Princess couldn't see how one dragon could penetrate the defences of the Ar'gon Tower.

Today the Princess and her captor were sitting outside the large tower watching the Junda play a ball game. If she hadn't been so engrossed in worry and thoughts of escape, Shari-Rose would have appreciated the giants' skill. The low gravity on Zanarah made the Junda quite weightless so they leapt and jumped to amazing heights. The game was played on platforms of varying heights with two opposing teams of six players trying to score a ball through their opponents' rings.

But the game was interrupted when the grey dragon was spotted circling the Ar'gon Tower. Only the magical Princess could see the wizards' shield enclosing the tower like an orb, preventing flying creatures from penetrating it. Now her keen elven sight saw the dragon fly low over the tall tower, and drop something small through the shield to land on the roof. Moments later, she could just make out the collapse of the two Junda guards on the parapets and realised that the intruder must have a bow and arrows. A halfling, she surmised, her heart racing at the thought that an ally had a broken through, perhaps one of the halflings she had met in the South Lands.

To divert the giants' attention, the Princess pulled on her leash and pointed at the dragon speeding over their heads to the east. "Look at that dragon," she exclaimed loudly and then gurgled as a sharp tug by Master Ab'hijit strangled her vocal chords. The Cyclops leader barked orders at his men, who abandoned their game and formed into a tight squadron of ten Cyclopes and almost one hundred Junda.

Five soldiers collected the fearsome Yarba beasts from their cages near the tower. These were hunting carnivores, the Zanarahn equivalent of bloodhounds, but were larger, broader and spiked. Shari-Rose had no doubt that they could tear the head off an elf and perhaps even a dragon. The animals were distributed one beast to twenty-five soldiers, who were sent out in five different directions to search, for Ab'hijit was determined to find and destroy the dragon and then kill Daeron, whom he decided was now a threat to the tower's security.

Meanwhile with her hopes rising, the Princess wondered who it was who had been dropped onto the tower's battlements. When would the dead bodies be discovered and a search of the tower ordered?

*   *   *

Sienna crept through the deserted halls of the tower with the stealth of a practised huntress. Sienna-Li flew nearby, looking into doorways and through windows.

"This is a bit too easy," murmured the little fairy in Sienna's ear. "I suspected my magic would get us through the shield, but this silence is creepy. Where is everyone?"

"Maybe they knew we were coming and got scared," joked the halfling in a whisper. "Honestly, I'm as worried as you. If not chasing us, does that mean they're hunting Asher or harming the elves? Many giants and wizards left yesterday with Shari-Rose's father, but we've seen at least a hundred of them exercising since then. There must be a few wizards left too, for the tower shields still hold. If there aren't enough wizards left to open a portal, then we're isolated here. Come on, let's keep looking for the elves."

Presently they came upon a stout metal-reinforced door. The little fairy peered through the large keyhole, discovering it was big enough to fly through. His tiny eyes widened in alarm at the sad sight beyond the door. Seven wizards surrounded a metal rack in the centre of the room, upon which were chained six Nnanelli women and a man covered in dried blood. One of the chained women hung limply and the wizards wept around her.

One spotted Siena-Li and exclaimed in surprise as he flew closer, "It's a Relorian fairy!"

One mage gestured to the woman's body. "The giants beat her to death because we could not reform the portal," he cried in anguish. "There are too few of us now. We're exhausted and will soon be too weak to maintain the tower shield. Was it you who came through the portal on the grey dragon?"

"Yes," replied Sienna-Li. He gestured towards the door, "My halfling is Sienna and we came to rescue you and the elves. Do you know where they are being held?"

Another mage spoke dejectedly, "There is no escape on this accursed planet. The villages are far across the swamplands, but we would be caught by their beasts before we got there and the village giants would not shelter us. We are not strong enough to reform the portal, so we are stuck here until another portal comes from Zumar, if ever. We don't even know how many wizards still exist since Nnanell was overrun by Vergai. We hold little hope of ever being rescued and may yet be killed when they realise we are not strong enough to make another portal. We are so weak they've stopped guarding our door."

The little fairy felt the wizards' frustration and wished he could help them. "We'll keep searching for the elves and a way to escape, so don't give up hope. We'll return as soon as possible to spare you the giants' cruel treatment." He reluctantly left the poor wizards and returned to Sienna.

Fairy and halfling continued their search, finally locating Daeron's prison cell. The door was guarded by a Cyclops and two Junda guards staring intently at the closed door as though the elf might materialise and attack them at any moment, which allowed the intruders to slip quietly down the corridor behind them.

Continuing on, they reached the large throne room seen in the vision back in Conlaoch Diarmada. The wide pillars supporting the castle continued through this vast room. The ceiling was lost in darkness far above, and the room took up most of the ground floor of the tower. Behind the throne was a lattice wall. Sienna noticed a broken piece of wood in the bottom and when voices sounded from the doorway, she squeezed through the broken lattice, hiding in a dark narrow space running the length of the wall. Sienna-Li followed her and she quickly whispered to him to extinguish his fairy glow.

They had barely settled into hiding when a large party of giants entered the throne room.

Looking through the lattice, Sienna saw Master Ab'hijit storm into the room with a face like a thundercloud, dragging Princess Shari-Rose by a thick rope around her neck. She was holding onto the rope with both hands and the halfling could see reddened marks around her slender neck and a desperate look in her eyes. Barely clothed, she wore only golden pantaloons and a narrow strap of golden cloth that covered little of her curvaceous chest and her red-gold hair was fashioned in a high ponytail, resembling the giant's scalp-locks.

She slumped dejectedly behind the throne to avoid the giant's attention, but he pulled on the rope and thrust her onto the floor in front of him.

"Dance slave," he commanded. The elf gave a small sigh, reached down to the floor and picked up small metal castanets called zills, sliding her slender fingers into the bindings. Beating the zills in a complicated rhythm, she swayed her hips slowly to the beat. The other giants clapped their hands admiringly to her rhythm and yelled for her to jump. As the audience cheered her on, she leapt high in the air and somersaulted to the ground with elven agility.

Master Ab'hijit sat on the Emperor's throne and watched her for a short time, then clapped his hands once. The elf abruptly stopped dancing and crept quietly to her place behind the throne. The giant leader barked out orders to the Junda, who scurried to obey. "Get my drink, fetch my food. Kneel before me for there is no link to Zumar now and I declare myself the new Emperor of Zanarah. You will find whoever has killed the rooftop guards and bring him and the dragon before me, dead or alive. My word is now law!" Most of the Junda left the room to search for intruders.

One of those remaining tentatively approached the throne, "But Master, you have sent most of our soldiers out with the Yarba beasts. Shouldn't we wait until the searchers return?"

"You dare to question me?" roared the self-proclaimed Emperor. "You will pay for your insubordination!"

Ab'hijit's large eye glowed red, then white hot and Sienna gasped as the beam tore up the large floor tiles and cut through the disobedient creature like a scythe from head to toe, the two halves of his body fell apart to the floor. The beam died and the new Emperor snarled, "Let that be a lesson to you all that my word will be obeyed without question."

There was a profound silence in the room as the horrified giants all stared at Ab'hijit in shock before falling to their hands and knees on the floor, cowering in obeisance of their new ruler. Ab'hijit gave a satisfied murmur.

Those remaining silently crawled backwards out of the room and the halfling and her fairy held their breath. Now alone, the new Emperor mumbling his frustration and the halfling and fairy settled in for a long wait.

Now the only sound was that of the new Emperor noisily eating and drinking. He threw a small crust of bread on the floor for Shari-Rose who grabbed it ravenously and began to eat.

Sienna-Li tentatively poked his head out from the lattice and seeing the coast was clear, flew towards the elf. She gave a small gasp when she saw him and then coughed quickly to cover the sound. The self-proclaimed Emperor meanwhile fell asleep, snoring loudly.

The Princess embraced the tiny fairy with a smile. But this turned to steely determination when she looked back to the throne with a look of pure hatred.

*   *   *

It was a long week, travelling through the snowy tundra of northern Reloria. The companions wearily huddled on their sleds against the bitter cold and the snow was falling so heavily they could barely make out the sled in front of them. Baja was leading but the top of his rich red hair was all that could be seen above a sled full of snow. Randir was just behind him and wondered how the dwarf could be snoring away with snow piled up to his beard and billowing around his face with every breath.

Behind Randir's sleigh came Fendi and Sir Jerephey, then Varnon and Raja speaking quietly together at the rear, each sleigh pulled by eight strong dogs. The white wolf ranged near and far, and at that particular moment was chasing an elusive rabbit through snow-covered trees. She panted with excitement, dashing and darting in hot pursuit of the nimble creature, but soon disappeared from Randir's sight in the falling snow.

His gaze returned to Baja in the lead sled and the clearing up ahead where trees bordered a large, open area.

Suddenly Baja's sled came to an abrupt halt when it ran into a snow-covered log. The dwarf was catapulted forward, snow spraying as he flew through the air and landed in a snow drift. All the riders immediately reined in their dogs sensing something was amiss. The dogs whimpered, but all eyes turned in unison to the small creature hovering above the groaning dwarf. Randir strained his eyes to see what looked to be a large white butterfly. The halfling coaxed his dogs slowly forward for a better look but a disembodied voice said, "Stop right there, you're all in grave danger!"

Randir looked around him, but saw only the heavy snow and the white butterfly. He climbed out of his sled, edging slowly towards Baja. The dwarf held up his hand in a halting gesture, but Randir's curiosity overcame his common sense. Approaching the dwarf's sled, he heard an unusual cracking sound and the ground shuddered beneath him.

"Back up slowly, you fool," the voice commanded. The white butterfly fluttered rapidly towards him and his fairy gasped in surprise, for the butterfly was revealed as an albino male fairy dressed in white hose and tabard. Randir was turning to obey the disembodied voice when the snow-covered ground shuddered violently and opened up at his feet. He had a split-second to see Baja cutting his sled's reins with a knife, before he was plunged into an icy lake.

The shock of the cold water almost stopped his heart for a moment, and gasping for air, he surfaced in a lake full of broken ice and panicked dogs. He began to hyperventilate, his heart pounding in his ears as he submerged once more, dragged downwards by his heavy clothes, bow and arrows. A wide-eyed sled dog pushed him further under, swimming past the halfling and trying to scramble onto the remaining ice. Two strong arms pulled the dog to safety and reached for Randir. He was beyond reach of the searching hands, but had the presence of mind to grab the bow strapped across his chest.

In desperation he disentangled the bow and held it above his head. He felt someone pull firmly on the bow, but black spots danced before his eyes, then his body went completely numb and he blacked out.

"Randir, Randir, can you hear me?" a far-away voice called him.

"He's gone into shock! Quickly, remove his wet clothes," a voice urged and his befuddled brain vaguely recognised it to be the same voice that had warned him to stop.

He shivered uncontrollably as strong arms were removing his clothes, his breath came in gasping pants. The white fairy fluttering above his head reminded him of his own bond fairy.

"Ran...dir...La," he managed to speak in between gasps.

Fendi's face appeared above him and he spoke, "She's all right Randir. You're going to be OK." He friend's face then turned away and enquired, "Have they found him yet?"

Randir was puzzled for a second and then, "Baja! Is he alright?"

There were a few tense moments when no-one answered him until Fendi turned back. "Yes, the snow-halflings are dragging him out now. He is blue and..." Fendi's voice broke off as he choked and turned away. Randir seemed barely able to move with the hyperthermia, and someone covered him in layers of warm fur blankets.

Randir turned his head and saw his fairy lying prostrate beside him with unfocussed eyes blinking rapidly as the snow fell on her. Further away towards the icy waters several small white-cloaked figures stood with his friends surrounding Baja's still body. They were stripping off his wet clothes and replacing them with large furs from a sled. One of the white halflings leaned over the dwarf and breathed air into his purple lips. After several anxious seconds, Baja spluttered, coughing up lake water. He took several breaths of the cold air and, declared, "Well, I think I've died and gone to Heaven. I'm surrounded by beautiful white angels and I can see a bright light."

"That's just the sun shining on the falling snow, you dolt," said Raja affectionately. His lightly teasing words were betrayed by the concerned frown on his brow. "I guess you must be alright if you're trying to charm your pretty rescuer."

Randir had a closer look at the small people with Baja and realised they were halflings like him, but pure white compared to his own mid-brown colouring, and their eyes were pink. Their hair too was long and pure white and they were covered in white furs from head to foot. He looked with envy at their warm attire for he was naked under the furs. Still shivering, he tried to find more covering and a tiny halfling woman noticed him squirming and came over to him. She was just a few years older than him, with long white hair hanging down in braids beneath a furred hat.

"Hush brown halfling," she said softly. "We need to warm you before you can be moved. You don't want to lose your extremities to frostbite." This thought sounded quite frightening and he instantly lay still. The young woman took off her own warm coat and lifting the edge of the fur blanket covering Randir, crept in next to him. She wriggled for a few seconds before settling with one bent knee lying on top of his thighs. He felt a strange mixture of excitement and curiosity when she sighed contentedly in his ear and wrapped her arms around him. At a loss for words, he lay very still and quiet in her arms.

Her skin was very soft and he could feel her heart beating. He was acutely aware of every place where their bodies touched and he tried to calm his rapid pulse and breathing.

After several minutes the bold halfling whispered in his ear, "My name is Ennis and this is my fairy, Ennis-Farry. He is trying to wake your sleeping Randir-Fae."

"Randir-La," corrected Randir automatically. "Is she alright?"

"I'm sorry," answered the snow-halfling. "All of our fairies are call 'Fae' for female and 'Farry' for male. I guess things are different where you live. I'm sure

Randir-La will be fine because you are well. You are bonded together are you not? When we pulled you from the water she came to the surface and we caught her too. Can you mind-speak?"

"I don't know what you mean by 'mind-speak," Randir replied, a puzzled expression on his face, for he heard Ennis repeat the question inside his head without moving her lips. He answered aloud, "Yes we are bonded and can heal and feed each other. If our fairy dies, so do we. We've never done this mind-speak before."

"Do not fear, for she is coming around," declared Ennis-Farry, his wings fluttering above Randir-La's head.

The snow stopped for the moment and Randir was able to study his rescuers. The fairy's wings were covered in intricate silver patterns and his hair and skin were as white as snow.

Randir pulled his head away from the snow-halfling cuddling up to him and saw that she was kind of cute, with a cheeky little smile on her lips and a faraway look in her strange pink eyes. She caught his gaze and he heard her voice within his head say, "Do you like me?" Her lips didn't move and he stared at her for several seconds before answering.

"Yes," he replied simply, "Although it is a strange way to meet, with me naked, freezing and dripping wet and you curled up beside me under many furs. Were you watching us come down the path on our dog sleds?"

Ennis blew gently in his ear and cuddled him tighter, speaking again mind-to-mind, "Well for one thing you weren't on the path when you tumbled into the lake. The ice won't be thick enough to walk on for another week or two. I think the dwarf was asleep and missed the track markers veering off around the lake." Randir followed her gaze to a series of upright sticks a short distance away. "Anyway, we were fishing by the lake just ahead of you. I saw you coming and called out to you with my mind. Surely you heard my warning?"

Randir nodded sheepishly, feeling embarrassed that he had disregarded the warning. "I'm sorry, I was looking for you and wondered why the dogs stopped. Are they alright?"

Ennis tenderly touched the side of his face and Randir felt pain there now that the feeling was coming back. He put his fingers to the skin and they came away with blood on them.

"Yes, all the dogs scrambled out of the lake," she replied. "One of them scratched you pretty badly in its panic to escape the icy water. Your chest is scratched as well and will need attention. Dorran has gone home to get some warm clothes for you and the dwarf. He will return soon and we will take you to the warmth of the northern outpost."

"The outpost?" repeated Randir in surprise. "Are we there already?"

Ennis kissed the throbbing side of his face and spoke telepathically, "Yes, we like to consider ourselves the guardians of the Northern Outpost, although really we just moved in when the wizards abandoned it. They left to build themselves another home still further north, which outsiders are forbidden to visit."

After a while, a rather sour-faced Dorran and another halfling returned, both carrying armfuls of warm clothes for Randir and Baja. The effervescent dwarf was regaling a crowd of snow-halflings with tales of their quest for the Elven Jewel. Dorran looked somewhat bitter at the attention being shown to the newcomers and dragged Ennis out from under Randir's pile of furs.

"Have you no shame, Ennis?" he hissed at her. "You are promised to me and yet you throw yourself at this brown stranger. Cease making a spectacle of yourself and return to the castle at once!"

Ennis surprised Randir by determinedly turning her back on Dorran and helping Randir don layers of warm clothes. "You can say what you like Dorran, but I will never be with you. Go and make another halfling miserable, for I won't have you."

Dorran gave Randir a look so fierce that he staggered backwards and was caught in Ennis' arms. The acerbic halfling then about-faced and stomped off in the direction of the castle.

"Thank-you for the clothes Dorran," called Randir, but his words were lost in the heavy snow. He felt annoyed that Dorran was blaming him for this, since he'd done nothing to encourage Ennis. But he did find her very attractive.

"Well, better be getting out of this storm," Ennis said in his mind. "We won't catch any more fish in this weather and you need warming in front of the fire. Don't worry about Dorran. He's upset because I keep refusing to marry him, even though we were promised at birth. Honestly can you blame me? He's awful and I hate him. All I want to do is leave this desolate place. Do you think I could travel with you for a while? It sounds as though you are having quite an adventure, listening to the dwarf."

"Yes, quite an adventure!   But the only place we are headed is trouble and sadly, there is no way that I can see for you to come with us." His voice dwindled away at the frustration he saw in Ennis' eyes.   He wished there was some way to help her, but knew his companions would never agree to take her.

CHAPTER 12: THE NORTHERN OUTPOST

After a difficult slog through the heavy snow, they arrived at the icy northern castle. As with the other three outposts, this one was an identical design, except made from blocks of ice instead of rock. Ennis explained that the wizard's magic kept the snow from melting even when there was a roaring fire in the hearth. The one difference Randir noticed in this castle was that instead of the centre courtyard being open to the air, there was a transparent steeply-gabled roof showing heavy snow falling above them.

They were met by Dorran's father Dreyfus, the mayor of this small settlement. He was polite and welcoming, but frowned at the way Ennis firmly held Randir's arm and showed him around the castle.

To Randir's great surprise, it was Violetta who managed to break the ice with their frosty hosts. After spending weeks as various creatures, the wizard's apprentice had now reverted to her human form. Looking as quirky as ever with black hair piled like a huge beehive atop her head, Vi's striking violet eyes somehow captivated the ill-tempered Dorran across the table.

"You're from Nnanell," Dorran declared in surprise, jumping up from his seat and racing around the table to greet her. To the hunters' quiet amusement, the snow-halfling bowed low before the apprentice and kissed her toes, followed by every snow-halfling present. Baja managed to turn a suspicious-sounding guffaw into a coughing fit and three pale halfling maidens jumped up to get him water.

Violetta seemed quite comfortable with this grovelling and bade the halflings rise, holding her hand in front of Dorran and drawing a circle around his head. His grumpy demeanour immediately changed to one of rapturous bliss, and he was seen to smile to himself for some considerable time afterwards.

Ennis thankfully embraced Violetta and the two of them were soon chatting away like old friends. It seemed that Violetta's aunt was the shield-holder of the northern region. Her name was Wizardess Aqualina and her talents were with shape and water, which explained the castle of non-melting ice. When Violetta asked to see her aunt, she was informed that Aqualina did not permit visitors, for she was far too busy with her work.

The young apprentice resolved to slip in to see her after dinner anyway.

Baja offered to entertain the mayor with some music and dancing, but sombre Dreyfus said he cared little for such pastimes. Baja was a little disappointed by this, but soon recovered his good temper and sang a love song to a fair snow-maiden, while Raja accompanied them on his pan pipes. The companions felt their aches melt away with the magical healing of the pipes and Randir felt the gashes on his face and chest tingling.

Sir Varnon and Fendi were chatting calmly to the mayor, who seemed pleased at the change in his son, and his opinion of the hunters rose considerably when he realised there was a wizardess among them. None of the companions thought it necessary to tell him that Violetta was a mere apprentice and a rather annoying one at that, for she had more than proven her worth to the group and they had all become quite fond of her, in her animal forms at least.

Violetta told Mayor Dreyfus that they intended leaving for the Wizards' Pinnacle the following day if the snow storm abated. The now jovial mayor, however, thought that it may have set in for a few days and insisted on the hunters staying at the castle until conditions were more favourable.

Fendi and Randir were intrigued to hear more of their destination, but Violetta withheld any further information except that only wizards were permitted entry. The halflings were disappointed, but knew that she would not relent on this topic, as being their guide was her reason for inclusion in the hunters' party. The conversation soon changed to Violetta's hairstyles and the young halflings moved across the room.

Ennis grabbed Randir by the hand and offered to introduce Fendi to some snow-halfling girls. Fendi looked around the room and his gaze met a pair of large pink eyes shining with anticipation. He gave a small smile, which dimmed at the thought of another pair of beautiful eyes, dark brown ones he might never see again. He broke off the exchange and shook his head at Ennis. "No thank-you Ennis, my heart lies with another halfling," he said. Ennis nodded and the three of them secretly left the great hall.

Ennis and Randir had to chuckle about Dorran's attraction to Violetta as they climbed the spiral staircase in the tallest tower. Randir was enjoying the snow-halfling's lively company and squeezed her hand affectionately. As they neared the top, Ennis paused on the stairs and whispered, "Our wizardess does not like to be disturbed, but I'm sure she would like to meet you because you've brought her niece along."

"Shouldn't we bring Violetta up with us?" suggested Randir, who did not want to be turned into a mouse by a stranger.

"She's right behind you," said a gruff voice, the three startled halflings turned to see Dorran and Violetta climbing up to meet them. "I think it's pretty rude of you to come up here without us, Ennis." Dorran was back to his grumpy self at the sight of Randir with his betrothed.

Randir blushed with embarrassment, but Ennis just laughed. "Oh you're just jealous because I thought of it first, Dorran. It is a good idea to bring Violetta up here though. Good for you Dorran."

To Randir's surprise, Dorran bowed his head and smiled at Ennis. "Anything to please you, my lady," he said sweetly. It was the first nice word Randir had heard him speak and it changed his sour disposition to quite a pleasant one. Randir wondered why Dorran was so bitter. He was a good ten years older than Ennis, but surely something must have happened between them for Ennis to despise him so. Randir tried surreptitiously to slip his arm out from Ennis hold, but she clung tighter

268

and smiled sweetly, causing Dorran glare at him again, and Randir wished he were anywhere but trapped in a tower between the two of them.

They climbed the last few stairs to the top room of the tower, and stood apprehensively on a wide landing while Ennis knocked. Instead of opening, the door simply disappeared and the halflings gasped at a beautiful garden in front of them. Their fairies gave squeals of joy and darted in amongst the fragrant flowers.

"Hmm ... uninvited visitors. Is the castle on fire? Do I need to pack my belongings?" said an irritated voice from somewhere deep in the garden. "I'll send some water to help with that fire and see you safely out of harm's way. Do be careful going down the stairs."

Without further warning or sign of the wizardess, a deluge of water poured over them, carrying them back towards the stairwell. Violetta rapidly shape-shifted into a fur seal and her lips mouthed another spell under the water as they were dragged along. Suddenly the flow of water came to a halt as though a wall of glass had been placed across the top of the stairs.

"I can't swim," Ennis gulped as she tried to take a breath and then sank under the water. Randir being a strong swimmer from living on the river in Southdale, held her chin above the waves crashing from wall to wall. Fortunately Fendi and Dorran were able to tread water.

The fur seal swam past them towards the garden and suddenly the water disappeared; not drained away, but merely disappeared. One moment they were swimming and the next they were falling to the wet floor.

"Well that was unexpected," the voice said from within the trees and a short, dumpy woman appeared, carrying a book and several flowers. Her grey hair hung down her back in a long braid. "I thought you would leave and here you are swimming in my garden. Which of you created the magical wall?"

"I did Aunty, with an air shield spell," declared Violetta proudly. She had shape-shifted back into human form when the lady appeared. "Aren't you proud of me?"

"Nnandarm's beard, it's little Violetta!" remarked Aqualina enthusiastically. "I'm certainly pleased to see you have come into your power. You were a late bloomer and Wizard Nnald is so doddery that I feared he wouldn't be able to teach you." Then a thought struck her, "You have both air and shape-shifter powers. Ohhh! Another double power in the family, that's wonderful. I have both water and shape-shifter powers and was the only double in our family before you. Wait until you go home and tell the family!"

As Aqualina walked toward them, the years seemed to melt away from her face. By the time she embraced Violetta, she was a young lady again. The two looked like sisters with their long black hair and pale skin, though Aqualina's bright aqua eyes contrasted dramatically with the violet ones of her niece.

"Just let me show you how much I have learned aunt," declared Violetta enthusiastically.

The wizardess and apprentice launched into a rapid conversation hardly pausing for breath, while the halflings exchanged knowing glances, quietly slipping away down the stairs. Ennis was holding tightly onto Randir's arm, grateful to him for saving her in the water, while Dorran grumpily followed them.

As they returned to the great hall Fendi remarked to Randir, "They'll probably be talking all night, so we might as well go have some fun. Her aunt is an amazing shape shifter."

"She's not very good at maintaining the shield, for she's not an air wizard. I bet she's trying to talk Violetta into doing it, when she completes her training and becomes a wizardess too," volunteered Ennis.

"She'd be lucky to get a word in," Randir replied with a smirk.

"Would you stay, if the apprentice does?" asked Ennis, who had not left Randir's side the entire night.

"I don't think we have room for any more halflings here," said Dorran rudely, prying Ennis away from Randir's arm. "My father wants to see you Ennis," he said half-dragging her to the long table. Ennis gave an apologetic look to Randir as she left.

"You're best not to come between those two," said Fendi, heading in the opposite direction.

Randir shrugged his shoulders. "I didn't ask for any attention," he protested.

"I know," Fendi replied. "She seems nice, but she'll bring trouble, that one. Dorran is pretty possessive."

"I think I'll enjoy punching that pale face if it comes to that," whispered Randir cheekily. "I wouldn't mind a little female attention for a change." He cracked his finger knuckles as they spoke.

Fendi shook his head and raised his hands in a peaceful gesture, "I'm staying right out of this fight. You're incorrigible, Randir!"

Randir smiled back as they greeted the other hunters gathered around the fireplace. Baja and Raja were bidding a couple of the maidens goodnight.

Sir Varnon and Sir Jerephey were in conversation with some snow-halfling elders.

"We shall be leaving for the wizard's castle in the morning," Varnon said. "Violetta spoke of a way to get there which avoids the blizzard. I am sending Sir Jerephey back to Varx Castle because it is doubtful we will return this way."

"I hope you youngsters haven't been getting into mischief," Baja smiled as the halflings joined the group by the fire.

"I doubt they know how to stay out of it," said Varnon in a rare jest. "This journey has been constant trouble one way or another since we first met. In a way I think it lucky Asher is not here, for snow-halflings are as distrusting of mountain men as knights. I just wish I knew what was happening on Zanarah and if our Elven Jewel is safe."

Randir was distracted from their conversation by the sight of Ennis peering around a corner and beckoning him with a pale finger. The snow-halflings had all retired to bed like obedient children when their mayor had indicated that it was bed time. The hunters had found this a bit dictatorial, but respected their culture and thought it a bit risky for Ennis to have returned after her curfew. Randir gave Fendi a quick nudge and excused himself.

The two halflings crept quietly across the dark courtyard to the stables where the horses and dogs were housed. Their fairies also held hands and flew without their usual fairy lights. All the stables were in darkness, except for a small room where a fire burned low behind shuttered windows. Ennis explained that this room was used for treating sick or injured animals and no-one would disturb them at night.

"So why are we here?" asked Randir naively, his heart was pumping hard with excitement.

The snow-halfling didn't answer him, but smiled while her fur coat fell to the hay-strewn floor. "Would you like a massage?" said her thoughts inside his head. She wore a thin red dress and her white skin shone in the glow of the firelight.

Randir gasped and instinctively looked down at the floor. He saw her bare feet walking nearer to him and narrow legs silhouetted in front of the fire. The outline of her lithe body showed a womanly figure, while her long white hair fell free in waves to her waist. Turning her head slightly the light shone on her strong jaw and full mouth and her strange pink eyes looked deep into his. Randir tried to calm his breathing and racing heart. He tried to reply, but had lost his voice, so gave a slow nod instead.

His mind was thinking, "Oh my God, can this be real?"

"Very real," came her reply inside his head. "Take off your shirt and lie down for me."

There was no argument from the brown halfling, as he lay face down in the straw next to the one single toadstool which had grown under the quietly dancing fairies. Ennis was sitting on his lower back, rubbing lotion into his skin, which tingled with anticipation. The massage felt wonderful as the deep rubbing strokes on his back relaxed his tense muscles. On the other hand, he felt more excited and alert than ever before in his 17 years. His experiences of clumsy kisses with southern halflings were vastly overshadowed by the passion generated by this intimate massage.

"Can I kiss you?" he tried to direct his thoughts towards her.

The pressure of her weight on his back eased and he rolled himself over and propped his back against a bale of hay. She drew close and snuggled into his lap. "Did you enjoy that?" her thoughts asked; a knowing smile on her lips.

Randir answered by wrapping his long arms firmly around her and kissing her passionately. Her lips were warm and soft tasting vaguely of peppermint. He pushed her long hair back over her shoulders and pulled his head back a little to admire her beauty.

"I guess that answers my question," she thought and ran her fingers through his hair as she returned the kiss. There was no further conversation as they embraced in front of the glowing embers of the fire.

*　　*　　*

A large grey dragon beat tired wings over the swampy landscape of Zanarah. For a week Ash dragon had been chased by Junda giants and the spiked Yarba beasts.

276

Every time he thought he had eluded them and rested in a copse of trees, the spiked dog-like beasts would find him and climb the trees, forcing him to fly further afield in search of safety. He was pleased that there weren't any laser-wielding Cyclopes in the hunting parties, as they'd grown bored after the first day, leaving the two-eyed Junda in charge.

Ash Dragon gave a small snort of smoke as he banked away from the Ar'gon Tower heading towards the eastern horizon. His massive wings carried him upwards across the Zanarahn swamp lands and far from his pursuers, who looked like tiny ants far below him. He had returned to the Ar'gon Tower each day since leaving Sienna on the roof.

He had seen the elven Princess emerge daily, shackled to the giant Cyclops who appeared to be their leader. Shari-Rose was well guarded by the giants and the grey dragon could see no means of rescuing her. She appeared a little thinner than usual, from his keen dragon's eyesight. His gaze lingered on her skimpy golden outfit, the skirt sat low on her rounded hips and the narrow top clung to her ample bosom in the humid air. Her crystal jewel was covered by a golden scarf.

The Cyclops leader regularly pulled on her chain trying to intimidate her in front of the Junda, who were training by wrestling with each other and every second day played the ball game on multiple platforms. Ash was pleased to see from her defiant posture the giants had not yet broken her fiery spirit.

He was more worried about the brave huntress who had gone into the huge tower and had not returned or sent any signal to him. He was also concerned over the fate of Daeron, who had been injured during the crash landing and now possibly killed by the heartless giants. The dragon had flown past two days ago when a group of six Junda giants were being punished for not capturing the dragon. They had been hung upside down from the ball-games' high goal-posts for several hours and had turned purple. He could only imagine what they would do to him if he was caught.

This brought Asher's mind back to the young halfling. As his massive wings beat steadily away from the castle over Junda stilt-villages, his mind wandered back to the last thing she had said to him. "Trust me. I've hunted worse prey than these lumbering behemoths. If we have any chance of success, you need to keep them busy looking skyward, whilst I try to free our friends. I'll be walking out those tower doors with the Princess very soon." Then Sienna had given him a quick hug and jumped nimbly onto the tower roof.

*   *   *

Asher was very successful in his attempts to divert the attention of General Ab'hijit, or self-proclaimed 'Emperor Ab'hijit' as he was now known. The Cyclopes and Junda alike were terrified of becoming the next victim of one of his rages, cowering low or avoiding him altogether. The body count was mounting from failed attempts to capture the dragon and the lightning creatures were being gathered to aid their attempts.

Many Junda and Vergai were working on something down in the castle basement, but Sienna hadn't been able to sneak past the guards to see what they were planning. Every evening the Emperor demanded an update on the progress, but didn't specify what they were building. Sienna was quite frustrated at not knowing what it was and suspected that they may be making a weapon to use against the troublesome dragon.

The huntress and her brave fairy had been far from idle during the week. They had discovered a very large store of food and were secreting supplies to Shari-Rose and the Nnanell wizards. The tower had only a small compliment of soldiers now compared to its usual force and the likelihood of the food being missed was slight. The food stores were large and several pantry rooms lay in the cool cellar beneath the large throne room.

As well as the food, there was a separate room of medicines. The labels on the bottles were written in the language of the Zanarahns, which consisted of squares and dots. Sienna was examining the green liquid contents of one jar when they heard voices approaching. Sienna-Li stopped his glow and they both hid behind some large barrels in a dark corner of the room.

Two of the Junda walked into the medicine store with a lantern, and closed the door behind them. "How's Mesk'henet progressing with the interrogation?" asked the first one.

"Much the same as before," grumbled the second Junda. "The elf seems resistant to the truth serum, but she keeps giving it to him. I think they'd get more answers out of him if they brought Ab'hijit's pet into the room. Chop off a few of her pretty fingers and the elf will be singing all his secrets in minutes."

Sienna-Li clapped his hands over his mouth to avoid crying out in alarm.

The first Junda continued, "I don't think Ab'hijit will be Emperor for long, if he keeps up this attitude. Keeping that elven girl as his toy is a mistake and people are starting to say that he doesn't want the portal to reopen. He doesn't want Emperor Chi'garu coming back and punishing him for the way he has slaughtered any Cyclopes who has opposed him." The guard began fiddling around with the medicine bottles as he spoke. He picked up a small bottle filled with orange liquid and asked, "Is this the truth serum?"

The second Junda leaned towards him, "No, that's the sleeping potion. The truth serum is the next one. It's a bit darker and reddish. Those Cyclopes don't teach us to read, but they send us to get bottles with writing on them. They're the dumb ones! I think we should support Mesk'henet when she mutinies against Ab'hijit. It's only a matter of time before she challenges him."

The first Junda appeared rather shocked at this news, "Would she really dare to do it? If she doesn't succeed he will kill her and all of her supporters."

"Just keep it quiet and I'll tell you when the plan is made. You won't want to be on the wrong side if it comes to a battle. I tend to think that everyone will support Mesk'henet because Ab'hijit is too mentally unstable to rule for long. Anyway, keep quiet about it. We'd better get back with this serum. You know how frustrated she is getting in the torture chamber and I don't want her being angry at us."

As two Junda guards left the room, Sienna and her fairy breathed quiet sighs of relief. "Well that was some important information we overheard," said Sienna-Li. He flew up to the shelf and sat atop a bottle of sleeping potion. "I think this sleeping potion might come in handy." He had started up his faint glow in the store room.

"Yes, thank-you," replied Sienna. She picked up the small bottle and put it in the belt of her huntress clothes. "Do you think you could sneak it into the guards' drink outside the torture chamber? We really need to get in there to speak to Daeron."

"Of course I can do it," said Sienna-Li confidently. "We're the best hunters on this swampy planet."

Halfling and fairy stealthily made their way back upstairs to the Daeron's prison, high in the tower. As promised, the small fairy easily drugged the lazy guards by pouring the potion in their drinks.

Less than an hour later they were in the room with the imprisoned elf, while the guards dozed by the cell door.

Daeron looked a mess. His eyes were swollen, his face haggard and his body covered in burns while his long white hair was matted with blood.

Sienna was appalled by the poor elf's state and gave him a comforting hug, but stayed well clear of his painful wounds. She told Daeron of her clandestine entry into the palace and that Asher was also here, distracting the Junda to give her an opportunity to find the elves.

Daeron only managed to pry open one of his bruised eyes and he gave a little moan. "It's good to see you Sienna. Have you come to my rescue?"

Sighing in frustration, she replied, "I couldn't carry you, I'm afraid. You are so much bigger than I am and there's nowhere large enough to conceal you, even if you could walk. I'm hiding in a small compartment in the throne room and it is down many flights of stairs.

"No," said Daeron sadly. "I am too weak from the starvation and torture. Have you seen dear Shari-Rose?"

Sienna gave him bread and cooked meat that she had found in the pantries. "Well at least I can bring you food and make you stronger to help you heal. The Princess is doing fine and is still quite defiant. The new Emperor is keeping her on a close leash as his pet, so we haven't been able to speak with her, but we're feeding her so she is regaining her strength now. We've been trying to get in to see you for a week and luckily we now have a sleeping potion to give your guards. We'll try to come each night to bring you food. The guards are lazy anyway, so if anyone finds them sleeping, they won't suspect anything.

"There is one piece of good news that we heard tonight: the other Cyclopes are annoyed with Ab'hijit and may soon challenge his leadership. This would give us some distraction to get you out of here. Sienna-Li and I will try to find somewhere to take you when that happens."

It was very frustrating that she could not rescue Daeron yet, but Sienna tried to keep a brave face in front of him. She kissed him gently on the cheek, and then slipped quietly out the door with Sienna-Li. The guards were sleeping heavily as she slipped silently past with the sleeping potion tucked in her belt.

When they were alone in a corridor, the huntress broke down in tears. "I can't save him, Sienna-Li. What are we going to do?"

The little fairy reassured her with a kiss on the cheek, saying, "There, there, my brave one. You are doing an incredible job, feeding the elves and wizards. When they grow stronger we will all try to escape together and we would be much stronger with the wizards' aid. Let's bide our time and hope that Ash or the bickering Cyclopes will provide a diversion so that we can escape. I only wish that I could do something to heal poor Daeron."

"I miss Raja and his healing pipes. I'm so grateful to have you, Sienna-Li, you're the best fairy I ever met," said Sienna and she gave him a little hug. "Let's return to the throne room and get some sleep. I'm exhausted."

CHAPTER 13: THE WIZARD TRIALS

The next morning the hunters gathered outside Wizardess Aqualina's room at the top of the tallest ice tower. Sir Jerephey had already left for the Diagro Plains with the dog sleds, so the Hunters of Reloria were now reduced to the blond knight, the dwarven brothers, two halflings and their fairies. Violetta was still inside the tower room with the wizardess.

Varnon knocked once on the door which disappeared as it had done for the halflings the previous night.

"Enter," commanded a stern voice.

The hunters walked slowly into the verdant jungle occupying the magically-enlarged room. Birds were chirping as the two fairies flew nearby to drink nectar from flowers, and two mermaids with long black hair and fish tails sat on rocks by a small pond.

"Come closer," said the mermaid with bright aqua eyes. "We've been discussing many things, young Violetta and I. She wishes to undergo the wizard trials at the

Wizard's Pinnacle today. I have decided to break with protocol and allow you all to enter the Pinnacle yourselves. You will be the first non-wizards to ever set foot there, apart from the Elven Queen."

The two mermaids wrapped long robes about them and the hunters watched with interest as their fish tails blurred into legs. The ladies excused themselves in order to dress.

Randir and Fendi wandered through the jungle, peering at a family of inquisitive furmals who copied every moment they made. Randir discovered a roll of vellum tucked in his belt. "Hey Fendi, look what I have found in my knife sheath. It's a note."

"I bet I know which snow-halfling has been writing to you," Fendi said with a smile. "I didn't see the two of you all night and wondered where you had gotten to."

Randir blushed like a beetroot and turned away from his friend as he unrolled the vellum, a charcoal drawing in the likeness of Ennis. There was writing on the bottom of the vellum which Randir struggled to read. "Un...un...unril..."

"Give me that," said Fendi, snatching the note from his friend. "You never could read worth a damn. It says,

'Until we meet again.' I take this to mean that your snow-girl is keen to see more of you."

Randir coughed nervously to clear his throat, which made Fendi laugh. "It's good to see you happy, Randir and she seems like a really nice girl. I'd be staying away from Dorran, though. He won't let her go without a fight and I think he'd be very spiteful."

Randir nodded, "Well, we'd better get back to the others. There's no time for romance today."

The halflings walked back to find Aqualina and Violetta standing where the door had been, tracing a large circle in the air with their wands while chanting in a mystical language. The air shimmered and rippled in front of them then smoothed out and frosted over, clearing to show a curling icy spire, twisting its way into the clouds.

"The Wizards' Pinnacle and the northern-most point of Reloria," explained Aqualina and reached out, expanding the edges of the circle with her hands until the picture completely filled the space where the door had been. "You will need to pass the wizard trials before you can return to Nnanell to seek help. Good luck, dear niece. I will try my best to maintain the shield of Reloria until you can come back from Nnanell with the wizards."

Violetta embraced her aunt and took a deep breath before facing the magical doorway with Sir Varnon.

For once in his life, the tall knight looked apprehensive, which made Violetta smile. "Come on Varnon, surely the wizards cannot be scarier than an invasion of Vergai and giants." She tugged on his tabard and led him through the portal. Randir, Fendi and the fairies hurried after them, keen to show that they were not afraid, while the dwarves brought up the rear.

The Wizard's Pinnacle was an architectural marvel stretching upwards from a tiny outcrop of rock precariously dangling over a high cliff, with the frozen ocean below. The rock looked as though it should have fallen centuries ago, but had been kept in place by the wizards' magic. The building itself was made entirely of ice like the northern outpost. Its circular base was only slightly bigger than a large farmhouse, but the structure rose up and twisted along its entire height of almost a mile.

As they approached, the thick clouds parted and the sun shone brightly on the companions.

"That's air magic. Was that your doing?" asked Raja looking at Violetta in astonishment. The little apprentice gave a secretive smile, which made the dwarf think that perhaps she'd hidden some of her talents from them. He held Violetta's arm and they led the hunters through the snow towards the towering spire, with the apprentice wizard gushing enthusiastically over her various talents, much to the chagrin of the hunters.

Baja whispered in Randir's ear, "Our Vi was hard enough to live with before we discovered that she was super talented. This is going to be unbearable!" Randir nodded in agreement and they all groaned at the non-stop talking.

"I think I'd pay for a spell to stop her talking," said Raja, with a cheeky smile. "I thought we weren't allowed to come to the wizards' castle anyway. Isn't it some big secret?"

"Part of the test requires bringing loved ones with you to protect during the testing," Varnon said. "Violetta's family are all in Nnanell, so I volunteered for us to be her defenceless subjects to protect. That means that you'll have to leave your weapons when we go in to the arena."

"I'd feel naked without my war hammer," said Baja and the others all agreed.

"Well, it's one step closer to rescuing the Princess and completing our quest," said the knight. "And it wouldn't hurt to have a powerful wizardess in our debt now, would it?"

The dwarves and halflings sighed in unison. "I guess there's no choice then," said Fendi. "Well let's get on with it, though I don't much fancy being used as bait and relying on her magical powers to save me.

They reached the icy door of the Wizard's pinnacle and saw it was closed. A large statue of a white bear stood upright beside it. Violetta knocked once on the brass knocker and the statue opened its eyes to stare at them. "Greeting apprentice, what brings you here and why do you bring foreigners?" rumbled his growly voice.

Violetta blanched, but tried to appear confident, "All is well, protector. I'm apprentice Violetta, here to complete my exams and these are my defenceless subjects. All is in order." Her attempts at being cheerful were quashed by a growl from the bear.

"Drop your weapons foreigners!" There was clanging of metal as swords, knives, axes, bows and arrows fell to the ground. The large bear stared directly at Randir who reluctantly drew the knife out of his right boot and dropped it in the snow with the others.

"You may enter now," the bear said. "This spire has been recently abandoned due to the fighting in Nnanell, so the tests will operate automatically. You start in the antechamber and select which power you wish to test before entering the arena. You may take more than one test, but note that there is no failsafe mage to watch your performance. If you fail the test, the lives of your defenceless subjects will be forfeited. Proceed when you are ready." The ice door swung open and the white bear closed his eyes again.

"If you fail, we all die. I don't like this game already," muttered Randir worriedly.

"Fighting in Nnanell," commented Fendi as they went in. "It sounds like our problems are mounting."

Violetta glanced briefly at him, the worried expression playing across her face quickly replaced by a look of steely determination. Holding her head high she marched forward into the spire with a straight back while her defenceless subjects exchanged apprehensive glances before following her.

Like all magical structures, the inside of the building was completely different to the outside, with a large room bordered by five coloured doors. Just inside the entrance was a table with five bowls which the apprentice studied. Then she drew out her white wand, selecting the bowl with the carving of a cloud and wind, she asked, "What do I do?"

"You must fill your chosen bowl with that power," replied a disembodied voice. "I cannot guide you in this quest. Make sure that you only choose a test where you have a strong power. The price of failure may cost you your life or that of your companions. Remember the solution to each puzzle is quite simple, but not always obvious at first. Good luck, apprentice."

"We have no fear of death, apprentice," Sir Varnon proclaimed in what was meant as reassurance.

"But just hope it doesn't come to that," Baja added quietly and his brother nodded.

Violetta murmured a spell and the air bowl filled with a miniature tornado. A white door slid open and Violetta beckoned the hunters to join her, holding her wand in front of her as she passed through the doorway. Inside was a large rocky landscape with no end in sight. The sky was a strange green colour.

"It looks like a hail storm is coming," shouted Raja, as a strong wind buffeted the companions from all sides. The white door had disappeared.

"I'm trying to blow it away," yelled Violetta, "but the clouds won't budge." She was murmuring spells and waving her wand in the strong gusts. Her voice was drowned out by hail pounding down around them and flashes of lightning split the sky. Thunder rumbled and crashed, and the companions huddled together, for there was no shelter here at all.

Violetta sent her own blasts of wind pushing hard against the clouds, but they were magically held in place. She even tried to create a larger tornado, but it swirled round and round in the air and had no effect on the storm. A look of concern crossed her face as she realised that this wasn't the correct tactic.

"What simple solution can there be?" she wondered to herself. "I can't make the storm go away, so there must be something else I can do with my air power. What do the wizards use their air power for?"

She thought and thought, whilst hail fell on her companions, who were crying out in pain and sitting on the ground with their heads in their hands. "I need to protect them......with a shield!" The answer sprang into her mind and in two seconds flat she had conjured the shield she had used every single day in the desert outpost. A clear force-field spread from directly above her and down around them like an inverted bowl. "Why didn't I think of that sooner?" she asked aloud.

"We're just glad you thought of it at all," Raja cried, as he inspected a bleeding wound in Sir Varnon's blond curls. "Varnon is injured, but I can heal him with my pipes." He brought them out from a hidden pocket in his clothes. His soothing music caused the cuts on their arms to heal and the gash in the knight's hair to knit together.

Violetta heaved a sigh of relief when a chime sounded and the clouds magically disappeared. A mini tornado appeared in the air next to Violetta, but all around them was still. The white door popped back into view and the hunters rushed as one to escape.

The mini tornado hovered just over the tip of her magic wand and she guided it back through the white door to the air bowl on the table.

The second bowl Vi chose had a picture of hills on it. When she made a flower dance its way from Fendi-La's hair into the bowl, a green door opened onto a grassy field bathed in sunshine.

The companions looked around apprehensively for any sign of a 'land' challenge. There were pretty wildflowers in the grass and a gentle breeze ruffled their hair.

"I wonder if you have to make something grow out of the ground," suggested Randir, trying to be helpful.

Violetta shrugged and after concentrating, she managed to make a blade of grass grow as high as her head. Nothing happened. Then she made an entire forest grow on the plains to their left, but still nothing happened. "It doesn't look as though you are in mortal danger in this test," she said.

As though this was a preordained signal, a shout was heard from a small hill to their right and suddenly a hundred Vergai foot soldiers were running towards them. Violetta's eyes widened and she was frozen in fear. The Vergai onslaught approached rapidly, morning star weapons raised to crush the hunters. The apprentice stood there stunned and immobile.

Varnon shook her roughly, "Vi, you must do something....NOW! We are defenceless and cannot protect you from this foe."

"Try a shield spell again," pleaded Baja.

Vi shook her head, "It isn't a land spell. I can't think of anything."

"Please try something," begged Randir, as the Vergai approached the last few yards towards them. The hunters could even hear the heavy breathing of the Vergai fighters and see the bloodlust in their eyes. They knew that unarmed they could not withstand them, but they valiantly stood in front Violetta, to protect her for as long as they could, their widened eyes the only indication of their fear.

Violetta stamped her foot in frustration and then it came to her….Land. She raised her hands high into the air and brought them down in a chopping motion. There was a loud rumble and the ground between the hunters and the Vergai dropped suddenly away, leaving a massive canyon, extending in both directions as far as the eye could see. The hunters stepped hurriedly backwards and watched as the Vergais' momentum carried them over the edge and down into the deep canyon.

The falling Vergais' screams seemed to go on and on. Randir and Fendi shuffled close to the edge of the ravine. The crevasse went down further than the eye could see and wisps of smoke rose upwards as though from the very core of the planet. "Whoa," they exclaimed in unison.

A chime rang and a rock appeared suspended in the air above Violetta. The hunters sighed with relief and retreated to the green door once more. The rock followed her wand back to the table to hover over the land bowl.

"I don't know if my nerves can stand much more of this," announced Baja, now more rattled than in any time during all their adventures. "You are definitely buying me a drink when we get out of this, Violetta." The apprentice gave a small smile, but still looked wide-eyed.

"Two down," she said quietly and picked up a bowl with waves engraved on the side. She pointed her wand up into the reaches of the icy spire and the hunters watched as a drop of rain fell into the bowl. "I'm sorry, but I think we are about to get wet," she said apologetically.

Varnon gave a wry grin and removed his fur coat, breastplate, tabard and boots. He stood there in only his leggings and the dwarves and halflings followed his lead. Randir placed the note from Ennis carefully on top of his belongings.

Violetta sighed wistfully at the fine display of muscles, which made them all laugh. She then turned and led the reluctant hunters through the open blue door.

This time it seemed as though they had stepped directly onto a sandy beach. They heard a roaring sound and were looking for the source when an enormous wave appeared on the horizon and rushed towards them. The hunters tried to join hands, but could not touch each other, for each was now encapsulated in a big block of ice.

Violetta felt her prison with her hands. The walls were clear and cool and she could see a small hole just above her, slightly smaller than her head. Her companions, even the fairies, were trapped in cubes of ice.

Worse still, the rogue wave was closing fast. More than ten times the height of a man it loomed over them and began to break. Slowly at first, then the whole wave crashed down on top of them. The companions tried not to panic, but water rushed in through the hole in the top of each icy prison. They tried to block the holes with their hands, but water poured in and each block of ice began to fill.

The ice prisons floated to the surface of the water with the captive hunters banging frantically on the sides hoping to break free, to no avail. They turned to Violetta, whose ice cage had surfaced upside down, watching helplessly as she struggled to right herself. The hunters saw that the water level in her ice cube was stable, because the air could not escape through the hole at her feet. The choppy waves were still spilling over the other ice prisons and the companions tried to push their prisons over as the waves crashed around them.

Violetta could see the perilous situation they were in, for even the fairies small cages were almost filled with water and they struggled to breathe through the hole at the top. She knew that if she didn't find a solution quickly, they would all drown.

What could she do? Racking her brain for spells to settle the choppy seas, she tried a calming spell, which didn't work, then she tried a spell to drain the water away which didn't work either. Then she was distracted by the sight of Randir-La's cage now completely filled with water and the tiny fairy was staring at her in panic.

If only she could send the wave back where it came from…

She waved her wand and tried to push a huge wave of water away from them. It seemed to work and she held the wave up with a wand gesture. The wave froze in mid-air like a giant icicle. Violetta was heartened by this and tried again raising her other hand, pushed the water up all around them, freezing it into place. The icy prisons crashed onto the sand and shattered, and the companions all lay on the beach, coughing up the water they had swallowed.

Randir-La was lying motionless next to Randir and neither one of them was moving or breathing. The fairy's brown hair was plastered across her face and the apprentice wiped it to one side.

Fendi crawled over and gave the fairy a tiny squeeze on the chest. Water spewed from her mouth and both she and Randir began to breathe again. Fendi-La gave her a big hug and handed her the belled green cap, which was lying nearby and the two fairies shared a tear at the thought of how close Randir-La had come to death. Relieved, Randir hugged his little fairy as well and they turned towards Violetta.

The chime sounded again and a drop of frozen water appeared in the air above the apprentice. The blue door reappeared and the companions wearily dragged their saturated bodies back into the ante-chamber, where the icicle followed Vi's wand to hang suspended above the wave dish.

Not surprisingly, it was the ever-hungry Randir who discovered a banquet of food laid out for them. With water streaming from his leggings, he ran across the room and picked up a warm roasted leg of pork. "Over here," he mumbled through a mouthful of the delicious meat.

"This is just what I need too," agreed Violetta as she slumped down into a chair in front of roasted chicken and potatoes. "I'm sure this magic uses a lot of energy, because I'm starving."

Raja asked Violetta if she still wanted to go ahead with the final two tests. "No one would think any less of you if you decided to stop now. We all know how amazing your talents are and you don't need to risk your life to prove it again."

Vi shook her head, "I'm not going to quit now Raja. Anyway, it's not my life that I put at risk, dwarf, but yours. Are you brave enough to continue?"

Raja back-peddled quickly for she had turned the tables on him. "Do we look like a group who are easily scared? I'm sure we are all up to any challenge." He gestured to the hardened fighters who nodded in agreement. The water was almost dry on their muscular chests though various scars were still visible here and there. Violetta smiled, appreciating the view and silently wishing they would leave their shirts off more often.

When the hunters finished eating, they donned their dry clothes, and with renewed energy returned to the table of bowls. Three of the bowls now had the victory signs of air, land and water above them. That left only the powers of shape-shifting and fire. Violetta fancied her chances in a shape-shifting challenge and chose that bowl next, transforming it into a miniature statue of herself. A brown door opened on the far side of the room.

Violetta was next to Varnon as they went to go through the doorway. The apprentice walked straight through, but the knight appeared to bump against an invisible wall. The others tried to go through, but the way was barred to them too, and when Violetta tried to go back the brown door silently closed.

"Well I guess I'm on my own this time," she murmured, studying her surroundings. She was in the middle of a colourful jungle of tall trees festooned with vines. There was an abundance of wildlife and beautiful flowers of many different colours and shapes.

Presently someone came towards her, a shape-shifter who changed from a mountain troll into a knight, then a giant who became an elf, before turning into a friendly-looking mage. He wore an ancient-looking purple robe with matching rumpled hat and his hair and beard were long and white. His friendly eyes were a purplish-blue colour.

"Hello apprentice," he said. "I am an illusion in the image of Grand Mage Nnarndam. Welcome to the shape-shifter challenge. This is the fun challenge and I do hope you enjoy yourself. Your family will be waiting for you outside for there is no danger here." Violetta breathed a sigh of relief.

"It is a simple test," he continued. "We will play a game of hide and seek. If I cannot find you in five minutes, then you'll win. I am very good at seeking, so please do your best to choose a form that I won't be able to spot. The simple things are often the best. You have five chances. I will give you five minutes to choose a shape and then the game will begin. Good luck apprentice."

He walked off into the jungle and Violetta racked her brain to think of a form. Looking around, her gaze settled on a nearby brown simial, a larger relative of the furmal, and after careful study, she shifted into that shape. She climbed high into the treetops and sat near where other simials were grooming each other. The mage soon came back and spotted her straight away. "You have the head a bit wrong, I'm afraid. Try again."

Vi's second attempt was a green and red bird and she hid in the upper branches of the tallest trees. Nnarndam took a little longer to find her this time and after checking from the ground, he levitated through the air. He came quite close to her and called out, "Caught you. You forgot to fly away. I do admire your plumage though."

A little disappointed, the apprentice changed her tactic. The next turn she changed herself into a tiny halfling fairy and hid inside a large yellow flower. She could hear the mage talking as he searched for her, saying that the five minutes were almost up, then he spied her. "Caught you again," he called happily. "There wouldn't be a fairy here without a halfling. Two more tries."

Violetta stamped her fairy foot in frustration. How could she possibly blend into this jungle and not be caught? She looked around again and her gaze came to rest on an enormous tree. She decided that this time she would hide in plain sight. It was a tricky task to change herself into a tree. She grew very tall, her arms spreading out into branches with leaves on the ends. She even grew some white flowers high up at the top of the canopy.

305

She had no eyes to see the mage, but seemed to feel his presence as he scoured the jungle, searching for her. Time passed extremely slowly and she struggled to hold her many branches in place. Two simials jumped onto a branch and she could feel their small feet scampering along the bark. It tickled! She held the branches as still as she could, but the leaves on the end were quivering as she struggled not to shake. Mage Nnarndam was onto her in a second and he levitated up to the jiggling branch. "A ticklish tree, I haven't seen that before," he said with a giggle. "You look quite authentic, but it is very difficult to stand as still as a tree. You have one more chance apprentice."

What could Vi do? He had instructed her to keep it simple, but nothing seemed to be simple in this jungle. She was watching some large ants climb a tree, when she stumbled over a small rock. How about becoming a rock? It just might work. She looked for a place where she wouldn't get stepped on and spied a mossy hollow at the foot of a tree. She squeezed herself down into a small mossy rock shape and sat at the foot of the tree waiting.

She didn't have any eyes or ears, but could feel vibrations from the mage's footsteps as he walked through the jungle, and she even felt vibrations from the air as he flew past. All she had to do was sit and wait and not move. The waiting seemed interminable and she almost drifted off to sleep. At length she heard the voice of the wizard calling, "It has been half an hour apprentice and I have still not found you. You must have the best hidden form that has ever been used in this trial. Please come out and show me, as I am dying to know your secret."

Violetta slowly grew back into her own form and stretched.

"Were you an ant?" he asked, eager to know her secret. "I must have checked just about every ant in this jungle."

Violetta smiled a knowing smile at having beaten the Grand Mage. "I was a rock," she said simply. She gave a chuckle as the mage stood there with his mouth open in astonishment.

"No-one has ever been an inanimate object before. I didn't even know that it could be done." He still looked surprised, but shook her hand with enthusiasm. "Well, congratulations wizard. You are one of the very few to ever pass my test." He shook hands with her and they both heard the chime sound and the small figurine of Violetta floated through the air towards them. It followed her back to the foyer where a round of applause greeted her.

"Only one more to go," Randir exclaimed cheerfully. The hunters were keen to get the final trial over and done with.

Violetta formed a flame in the final bowl and the red door swung open. They all trooped forth into the last arena. This landscape was black volcanic earth and they could see Flame Mountain in the distance, with fiery lava oozing down the mountain side and smoke billowing from the crater.

A circular target was suspended in the arena quite a distance away and above head height. Violetta gave a grin and formed a ball of flame in her hand. She walked several paces forward, threw it as hard as she could at the target, which disintegrated. "That was too easy," said the apprentice and wondered if that was the entire challenge. Her moment of triumph was short-lived.

A screech sounded behind her and she swung around to see two large blue hydras carrying her companions away through the air.

The hydras looked exactly like spiteful Hydrane from Flame Mountain, with bright blue scales, multiple long-necks and tufts of rough hair on their heads. One was the colour of a summer sky and had two heads, the other a dull greyish-blue with three fierce-looking horned heads. Violetta watched in horror as her defenceless companions were quickly carried towards the mountain. She could hear their cries as the beasts' sharp talons dug into their flesh.

With little time to ponder their loss, an even larger two-headed hydra with midnight blue scales and enormous wings swooped down upon her. She had enough presence of mind to cast a ball of flame in its direction and it retaliated by expelling poisonous fumes and green acid at the apprentice. Thankfully these missed and the creature flew off before pausing some distance from Vi and staring at her with shiny silver eyes. "You are dead, wizard," it growled in a deep throaty voice."

Calming her nerves, Violetta decided to take the offensive. Her hand erupted into a sword made of flames. She spun it several times to test its weight and settled herself in a fighting stance, feet apart and knees bent. "Come and fight me if you dare," she challenged her winged adversary.

The beast snorted green fumes from its nostrils and retorted, "No-one has beaten me in seventy years, little girl. Do your worst and die with all of your friends."

The mention of her companions raised Violetta's temper. She threw bolt after bolt of fire at the great hydra as it swooped down. When the beast was almost upon her, she made the sword grow larger and swung with all her might. The flame scraped along the underside of the beast, leaving it blackened and charred. It roared in pain and anger. "You'll pay for that!" it growled angrily.

The beast changed direction and flew along the ground towards her. Violetta sent fire balls whizzing towards it but they exploded on the ground as the hydra swerved in anticipation. It blew a large cloud of poisonous gas in her face and she felt the acid burning her skin. Gritting her teeth she held her breath as she swung the flaming sword upwards. The fire sliced deeply through the hydra's belly and the great beast crumpled to the ground on top of her. An enormous dark wing was the last thing Violetta saw before passing out.

*   *   *

"Vi, Vi, wake up," said a concerned voice and she could hear the pan pipes music. The young apprentice tried to shrug off the fog in her mind and open her eyes. All she managed was a slight twitch of her eyelids and a long moan.

A wet cloth placed upon her forehead felt nice and cool after the heat of Flame Mountain. She could still feel a burning ache in her cheeks, but not as painful as before. At length she was able to open her eyes properly and squinted at the glare and the blurry figures surrounding her.

"Well done Violetta, you vanquished the monster. You were victorious!" said the voice, which she recognised as Sir Varnon. He was gently wiping the cloth across her brow and Raja played his healing pipes nearby. The fire arena had disappeared and she was back in the foyer room with the table and elemental bowls.

"How long have I been asleep?" she asked.

"The dying hydra fell on you nearly an hour ago, milady," the knight replied, "the rest disappeared when you conquered their leader. We were stuck up in the hydras' nest upon the mountain and it took a while to climb back down to you."

Vi saw that the dwarves, halflings and their fairies were all safe and sound. Raising her head off Varnon's lap she tried to stand, so Baja and Raja each grabbed one of her hands and hoisted her to her feet. As she thanked them, she saw a small flame hovering nearby.

"I did it!" she exclaimed. "I passed all five of the tests."

The hunters gathered around to congratulate her.

"Well done, we knew you could do it and are honoured to have you as a Hunter of Reloria, for you clearly are the mage we sought," said Sir Varnon. The others agreed with words of praise and congratulations.

The air shimmered in front of Violetta and the image of Grand Mage Nnarndam appeared. He smiled proudly at her and spoke, "Congratulations my great, great, great granddaughter, Violetta Nnarndam. I don't know if you realise this, but you are now the most powerful Nnanell mage of all time. You are the only wizard ever to have all five powers and you will be Grand Mage Violetta! There are only three living mages with three powers, including myself. I will await you on Nnanell and will be delighted to name you the new Grand Mage of our people."

Nnarndam faded like a mist and was soon gone from sight.

The hunters took a step backwards as the five elemental symbols floated in the air and hung suspended over the almost overwhelmed Vi's head.

The new mage looked at each element: air, land, water, shape and fire and they began to spin in a circle above her head. Spinning faster and faster they seemed to pull closer together as they turned. Soon it became impossible to distinguish the individual elements, for they were now a blur of white-hot light.

Violetta blinked rapidly, then shielded her eyes when the light became unbearable, glowing like a supernova. On impulse, she raised her wand high above her head and the elements elongated her wand into a glowing staff. As the light dimmed she saw the staff was made of solid silver, with a large shining diamond at its peak and the five elemental symbols were carved along its newly-forged handle.

The hunters knelt in honour of the new Grand Mage. Raja spoke, "You are indeed a mighty mage, Violetta; the greatest wizard of all time. Come and let us take the door to Nnanell to save our people and find a path to the Elven Jewel." The hunters gathered their weapons which were lying on the floor and prepared to follow her.

Mage Violetta nodded silently and the hunters watched as she traced a circle in the air with her silver staff, muttering the spell under her breath. The air in the circle rippled and a vision of a strange country appeared like a picture. With a small motion of her staff, the circle expanded to form an oval doorway.

The companions now looked at the bizarre scene before them of pink and orange rocks piled up in high columns. In the distance, blue and purple trees stood on either side of an impossibly tall white spire identical to the ice spire they were inside.

"Nnanell, my home," Mage Violetta said and led her companions through the gateway to the home of the wizards.

Epilogue: Dragon's folly

Asher had been very busy for the past few days, creating diversions for the giants. He had turned the tables on the teams of Junda and Yarba beasts who were chasing him and was now finding and destroying them from the air. He had discovered that while the Junda were excellent hand-to-hand fighters, they had no defences against an airborne attacker. Likewise the spiked Yarba beasts could climb and jump with ease, but could not catch the dragon as it flew past hurling balls of flame at them.

Ash had eliminated four entire search parties with his aerial assaults and now there was only one team of twenty Junda and one drooling beast left, and that team had gone into hiding in a Junda village far from the Ar'gon Tower. Dozens of wooden village houses were built on stilts suspended over the damp ground which flooded twice a day. Ash had spent a day waiting for them to emerge before deciding to return to the tower and leave them there. His diversion tactics had worked well and now one hundred less giants and four less Yarba beasts prowled Zanarah.

On the journey back to the tower, he pondered on what may have happened there during his absence. He knew that Sienna was a good huntress and she and her fairy had a good chance of evading detection inside the tower and bringing aid or rescue to the imprisoned elves. For this reason, he'd decided to return to the tower, to see if he could make contact with her.

Approaching the Ar'gon Tower, the dragon's keen eyesight made out the Elven Princess standing alone on the roof. He was sure that this was a trap, but he'd been here on Zanarah for many days now and this was his first chance to attempt a rescue.

Shari-Rose looked as beautiful as ever, with her long pony tail blowing in the breeze and she still wore the revealing midriff top and golden pantaloons. The wind blew the scarf hiding the crystal-rose jewel, and he caught a glimpse of it shining in the orange sunlight. The light caused a kaleidoscope of rainbows to radiate out from the jewel and hurt his sensitive dragon eyes. Her chin was lifted as she scanned the skies and finally saw him fly closer.

The elf appeared to panic at the sight of the dragon and waved her arms, pointing far off to the north. She shook her head and appeared to call out, but he could not hear her. Increasing speed, his wings beat strongly as he swooped towards the tower.

The frantic elf gave one more attempt to send him away and he was upon the tower. He snatched up Shari-Rose before realising that she was chained by the ankles to four separate stone blocks built into the castle. Putting her down again gently, the dragon gave a screech of rage and leapt onto one of the thick chains with his sharp talons, vainly trying to pull it out of the tower wall.

"Fly, fly, please Ash!" sobbed the Princess, but it was too late.

A Cyclops giant appeared at the top of the stairs in front of the dragon and Ash could see other giants surrounding him in his peripheral vision. The dragon used a fire bomb to incinerate the first giant and started to whip his barbed tail at the other giants. In that same moment, a huge metal net was thrown over him and the weight of it flattened him against the stones.

Watching helplessly, he saw Shari-Rose unchained and the collar replaced around her graceful neck. She was calling out his name and struggling in desperation as she disappeared from his view down the stairs.

Several Vergai now appeared in the dragon's view, holding onto thin chains extending high into the air. Hunched over, as if expecting someone to strike them, they began to fix the chains onto his metal restraints. From his viewpoint under the chain net, Ash couldn't see what was at the top of the chains. Roaring and breathing fire on the Vergai, he incinerated those he could reach.

He stopped abruptly when a bolt of lightning raced across the chains and paralysed him. His breath stopped momentarily and pain coursed throughout his body.

Ash's vision blurred and when he could see again, the leader of the Cyclopes was standing in front of him. Ash's gaze was drawn down to the elf beside the giant. Shari-Rose's big green eyes were full of concern and she looked as though she was trying hard not to cry. The Cyclops gave a yank on the rope around her neck and the Princess' face turned red as she was choked. The dragon tried to send a burst of flame at the giant, but only a faint wisp of smoke came out of his nostrils.

The Cyclops laughed at him and spoke in the language of Zumar, "Well dragon, it appears that you are defenceless. I am Emperor Ab'hijit of Zanarah and you are my prisoner. Unfortunately for you, I have enough prisoners already and have no use for you. But it will fun to watch you die, so I will leave you here. I might even come to visit you each day to see how you are going. It will be a slow and extremely painful death for a large creature like you to be killed by the Ildirim. They are the floating beasts above you, who make random lightning bolts. Well, now I have to be getting back to patting my pet here." He patted Shari-Rose's hair before yanking harshly on her leash. "Farewell dragon," he called mockingly and laughed as he dragged the struggling Princess away.

Another bolt of lightning crackled through the chains and Ash's yellow eyes widened with pain before he passed into unconsciousness again.

The end

Hunters' Quest

320

The adventures continue in …..

Dragon's Revenge is the thrilling conclusion to the Hunters of Reloria trilogy.

Coming in 2014

Check the website for details:

www.huntersofreloria.weebly.com

Dragon's Revenge book cover by Scott Patterson

The Hunters of Reloria book series

Hunters of Reloria logo by Bill Fox-Taylor

Also available is:

Hunters or Reloria series, book 1: Elven Jewel

Available in eBook and paperback

Book reviews:

If you have enjoyed reading Hunters' Quest, please recommend it to your family and friends and consider posting a review online. Kasper Beaumont is a self-published author and relies on word-of-mouth reviews and recommendations to tell people about the exciting world of Reloria. Many thanks.

About the author:

Kasper Beaumont was born and raised in Australia and lives a quiet life with the family in a seaside town. Kasper has combined a love of fantasy and a penchant for travel in this first series. Kasper started to write on the urging of friends and family and enjoys watching readers become immersed in the magical world of Reloria.

The Hunters of Reloria series are:

Elven Jewel

Hunters' Quest

Dragon's Revenge.

Website: http://www.huntersofreloria.weebly.com

Facebook: www.facebook.com/huntersofreloria

Twitter: https://twitter.com/KasperBeaumont

Made in the USA
Charleston, SC
26 April 2014